Out
of the
Dragon's
Mouth

Joyce Burns Zeiss

Woodbury, Minnesota

First Edition
First Printing, 2015

Book design by Bob Gaul
Cover design by Lisa Novak
Cover image: iStockphoto.com/7283342/©NuStock
Malaysia Map by Llewellyn Art Department

Flux, an imprint of Llewellyn Worldwide Ltd.

This is a work of fiction. Names, characters, places, and incidents are either the product of the author's imagination or are used fictitiously, and any resemblance to actual persons living or dead, business establishments, events, or locales is entirely coincidental.

Library of Congress Cataloging-in-Publication Data
Zeiss, Joyce Burns.
   Out of the dragon's mouth/Joyce Burns Zeiss.—First edition.
      pages cm
   Summary: After the fall of South Vietnam, fourteen-year-old Mai is forced to flee to a refugee camp on an island off the coast of Malaysia, where she must navigate numerous hardships while waiting to be sponsored for entry into America.
   ISBN 978-0-7387-4196-3
   [1. Refugees—Fiction. 2. Emigration and immigration—Fiction.
   3. Survival—Fiction. 4. Vietnamese—Malaysia—Fiction.] I. Title.
   PZ7.1.Z44Ou 2015
   [Fic]—dc23
                                                    2014041437

Flux
Llewellyn Worldwide Ltd.
2143 Wooddale Drive
Woodbury, MN 55125-2989
www.fluxnow.com

Printed in the United States of America

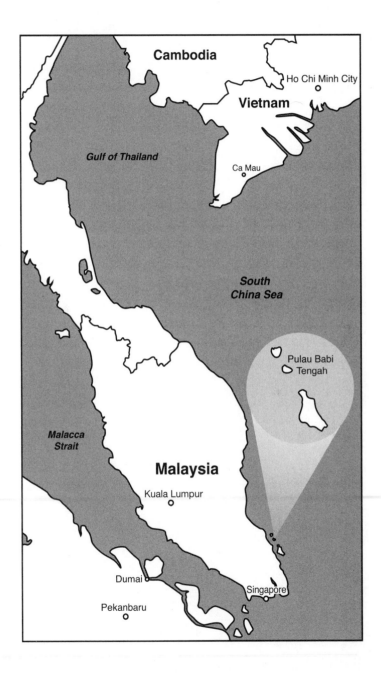

To the Vietnamese boat people

One

The darkness covered Mai like a burial shroud. She huddled in the small space allotted her, crushing her knees to her chest, struggling to breathe. The sickly smell of diesel fuel and the stench of human sweat engulfed her. Around her pressed a mass of human shapes, and a heat so heavy she thought she would faint. Soft moans and nervous whispers sifted through the stagnant air.

Above her, through a small opening, was a slice of blue sky, a whiff of the sea. She gasped and exhaled. The screech of the engines pierced her ears as the last refugee squeezed into the hold. Then she felt the fishing trawler rock against the waves, chugging down the river. She choked back a sob.

A crewman with a jagged scar on his bare chest peered through the hatch opening. "We're nearing the ocean," he cautioned. "Stay out of sight until we get past the patrol boats. Not a sound." The hatch cover dropped. Someone coughed. Then there was silence except for the sloshing of the waves.

Where were they going? Somewhere across the ocean—far away from Vietnam, far away from her family and home. Father had mentioned Hong Kong and Malaysia as he told her of the refugee camps. "From there, the Red Cross can help you get to America," he had said. "And soon we'll join you." She could still see his eyes, dark and desperate. Hong Kong. Malaysia. Strange names that meant nothing.

Father, father, I don't want to go.

You have to, he had told her. *You have to go to survive.*

But what if I don't survive, she thought. *You're not here to help me.*

She wished she were near Uncle Hiep, Father's youngest brother, but he was somewhere in the back of the boat. Dear Uncle Hiep. How she loved him. Even though he was nineteen, five years older than her, he was her favorite uncle, the one who paid attention to her when her parents were too busy. He lived in the family compound in a long house next to hers, and he always had time for her. When they'd arrived at the trawler earlier that day, he'd found her this space in the bow near the hatch.

She lowered her head between her knees and pushed her nails into her calves. The small red bag containing *banh te*, a mixture of rice and beans wrapped in banana leaves that Mother had packed for her, sat wedged between her feet. She felt the waistband of her loose pants where Mother had hidden two gold bracelets.

"These will bring you good fortune," Mother had said, pushing the needle through the soft fabric. "Don't tell anyone." Mai remembered how her mother's long black hair fell forward, hiding her sunken cheeks and her tired eyes. She seldom smiled these days, her brow always furrowed and her words short and few. Mai longed for the touch of her mother's hand on her cheek or a warm embrace.

The rough arms of an old woman pressed against her, and Mai felt a sharp elbow digging into her back. In front of her, a mother's arm enfolded her young son. He peered at Mai, his cheeks flame-red, his listless head propped against his mother's shoulder. Arrows of sunlight revealed the shadowy presence of a sea of heads and bent backs, packed like fish for market. A woman sobbed in the dark behind her.

Mai bit her lips until she could taste blood.

The drone of the engines suddenly stopped and she heard sharp voices overhead and the clump of heavy boots. The soldiers were on board, inspecting the ship. She held her breath and prayed. If they were caught and jailed, who would know where they were?

The baby next to her started to wail. She could feel the mother's arm when she raised her hand to muffle its cry. She waited to be discovered. The voices above grew louder. For a moment, she hated that child. Would all be lost because of one cry? A long silence. The boots clumped away, and the engine resumed its steady hum. Mai exhaled. *They've gone. We're safe.*

The hatch cover lifted. Fresh sea air and sunlight painted the hold. The crew man shouted down, "We're in international waters now. We've made it." A song broke out.

The rice Mai had eaten for breakfast started to rise in her throat. The plastic bag—where was it? Everyone had been given one. Now she knew why. She shoved it over her lips just as a stream of yellow liquid spewed forth, leaving a foul taste in her mouth. She wiped her lips with the back of her hand and gagged. Nothing came up. Oh, to be out of here.

The boat lurched, plowing through the sea while Mai covered her ears to block out the wails from the men, women, and children packed in this prison. The pungent smell of vomit filled the air and small pools of liquid puddled on the rough planks beneath her. Finally, the water grew calm. The incessant rocking ceased. The hold grew silent.

She thought of what Father had said about October. "It's a good time, the end of the rainy season. Fewer boats will be out looking for escapees in this weather."

She hoped he was right. It seemed much longer than two weeks ago that she'd overheard Father and Mother talking while she was lying on her mat in the storeroom they shared at her grandfather Ông Ngoai's textile factory.

"I've saved enough gold to get two out. Hiep's got to go now." Father's voice was low. "The Communists will send him to fight in Cambodia."

"Send Loc with Hiep," Mother pleaded. "They're taking fifteen-year-olds now too."

Mai had shuddered to think of her studious elder brother fighting.

Several days later, her father told them of the secret plan. "Hiep will leave with Loc and the rest of the family will follow, a few at a time, as soon as the passage money can be obtained." He ran his hand through his short, thick hair. "A fishing trawler, captained by my cousin, will be waiting to take Hiep and Loc across the South China Sea."

This was the only way. The new government of Vietnam would allow no one to leave.

Mai had felt relieved yet frightened. She'd heard stories of

Thai pirates who attacked refugee boats, robbing, raping, and killing, of boats that sank in raging storms, drowning everyone. She was glad they were sending Loc instead of her. Then she felt guilty. What if something happened to Loc? Her parents' hearts would be broken. Oh, she was such a bad girl. But she couldn't help the way she felt. She didn't want to go.

But the night before he was to leave, Loc had complained of a sore throat.

"You feel like a hot coal," Mother had said, placing her hand on his forehead.

Father looked at him and said, "The journey will be hard. You'll have to wait."

Mai had stared at her bowl of rice, waiting for his next words.

"Mai will take Loc's place."

A glob of rice had lodged in her throat. Shocked, she had thrown down her chopsticks and clutched Father's hands.

"I don't want to go without you," she cried.

"You're in danger, too. Even fourteen-year-old girls like you are being forced into the army now." The veins in Father's short neck bulged.

She clutched his hands and pleaded, but Father's face was unmoving, like the stone Buddha statue in the temple where they went to celebrate the Moon Festival.

She had never been away from her family. The daughter of a wealthy rice exporter, she had spent her life on the Mekong Delta near Can Tho, playing with her brothers, Loc and Quan, and her two sisters, Tuyet and Yen, along the river.

"Mekong means 'river of nine dragons,'" Father had told

them. "It flows from far away in the mountains of Tibet." He pointed to a map.

The war had been raging for as long as she could remember. The Americans had come to South Vietnam to help them fight for democracy. North Vietnam, under its leader, Ho Chi Minh, a funny-looking man with a long white goatee, was trying to take over South Vietnam and make Vietnam all one country. But North Vietnam was Communist, and Father shook his head. "We don't want to be Communist. We want to be a democracy. Why don't they leave us alone?"

In the blackness of the boat's hold, Mai prayed to her great-grandfather's spirit for protection. His picture had hung above the incense burners at their family altar in the large house they shared with Father's parents. He looked rather forbidding with his goatee and his bushy eyebrows, but he must have been handsome in his youth because he had managed to win the hand of the mayor's daughter.

Mai remembered her father telling them how Great-grandfather had fled the Communists in China and come to Vietnam, where he had worked for the mayor of the province as his bookkeeper. Because he had been so trust-worthy, the mayor had allowed him to marry his ninth daughter and had also given him much land. This land had now been in their Chinese family over four generations. "Please, Great-grandfather, protect us," she murmured.

Mai felt a painful pressure in her bladder. She'd tried not to drink too much that morning, but by now it must be afternoon. She could hear a voice from above, calling people up to the deck in small groups.

"You, come on. Get up here," ordered one of the crew.

Mai tried to stand, but her legs crumpled like wooden stumps. Sharp needles shot through them. She struggled through the hatch. Sun-blind, she swayed with eyes closed. A metal cup brushed her hand. Through half-open eyes, she could see water in it, could smell its wetness. She raised the cup to parched lips and let the warm liquid trickle down her throat. Opening her eyes wider, she could see tiny palm trees dissolving, the coastline slowly shrinking. The emerald-green sea swelled beneath her. Over the bow, a dappled sky.

Hiep, along with several other young men, was relieving himself over the rail. Several women and children formed a line by the rail behind the engine house, where a small box was suspended on a rough plank over the water. Mai joined them and watched as a young girl climbed into the box and sat down, her head poking up above the edges.

The pressure in Mai's bladder was unbearable. When it was her turn, she climbed over the edge of the box and pulled her pants down. Squatting on the plank with the hole in it, Mai peered down at the waves rolling below. A gush of warm urine shot from between her legs. She kept her eyes lowered, trying not to look at the people waiting their turn.

She remembered the day the pimply-faced young Communists clad in black shirts and pants, wearing *dép*—flip-flops—made out of old bicycle tires, had come to Rai Rang to take their house. Such peasants. They'd looked more like farmers than soldiers. They had never seen an indoor toilet. They caught fish from the river and deposited them in the shining toilet bowl to keep until they were cooked. How could such backward people have won the war?

Two

Hiep was waiting for her at the bow near a pile of fishing nets. "Mai, are you all right? I wish we were closer together."

"Yes, Uncle," Mai answered, watching the waves slap the side of the boat.

"Ahh," he said, taking a deep breath, "the air smells good." His bare chest expanded and relief spread on his weary face.

"I was so afraid when the soldiers came on board," she said, hoping he would not think her a coward.

"Bribed, paid a lot of money to let us go," Hiep said, resting his hands on his slim hips. "That's why our passage cost so much. They got their gold. And they left us alone. They knew the hold wasn't full of fish."

"Oh," said Mai, reassured. *That means they won't be back, doesn't it?*

"Time to go below," a crew member called.

So soon?

"Here, let me help you," Hiep offered. He slid into the hold ahead of her and caught her when she jumped down. His arms felt strong.

"Thank you," she whispered. She slipped from his arms and pushed through the crowd to her space, where she squeezed in between the old woman and the girl with the baby. She clutched her arms to her knees. She yawned. Her eyelids drooped. She tried to sleep, but she was able to doze only for minutes.

That night, the wind grew in force until its howling surrounded the trawler like an army of ghosts. Waves washed over the deck and drenched the frightened refugees, battering the sides of the ship like angry fists. Mai could hear the wooden planks creak and groan under the onslaught of the storm, the joints straining as if the boat would splinter apart. In the hold, the constant chanting of prayers poured out around her, babies cried high-pitched wails, and children screamed for their mothers.

The storm raged until the morning. And then the wind died, the waves diminished, the rocking ceased. Mai emerged from the hold and, tilting her head toward the storm-washed sky, whispered thanks to Great-grandfather for saving them. Hiep, his face drenched in sweat, offered her a cup of water. Mai took a sip.

Wails came from below deck. Mai watched a distraught young man lift the limp body of his lifeless wife through the hold and lay her on the deck. Mai had never seen a dead body before. She gasped when the captain and his crew wrapped the woman in a torn sail and slid her overboard. Her stomach turned at the sound of the sharks churning through the water to devour the corpse.

"Don't look," Hiep said, pulling her away from the rail.

Mai's eyes closed and exhaustion flooded her body. *Please, Great-grandfather, no more storms. Bring us safely to freedom.*

Suddenly the engine stopped and she could feel the boat drifting. She heard shouts from the crew. "What happened?"

"Engine's dead," announced the captain.

The boat drifted for a whole day while Mai prayed for a miracle.

On the morning of the third day a school of dolphins frolicked alongside their boat, their fins slapping against the waves, their bodies glistening. For a while she watched them, but then they turned away, and she waved her arms and cried for them to come back. But they didn't.

That afternoon she sat on deck with her uncle. The rail was lined with men fishing. Her mouth watered at the thought of fresh fish. The trawler stretched on the surface of the silent sea like a dead bird, its heart no longer beating, its powerful wings rendered useless. From the water's depth, a whale emerged, a spout of water shooting from its blowhole. The fishermen cheered. Good luck was theirs.

She scanned the horizon, watching for the whale to reappear. A dot in the distance, moving toward them. Mai rubbed her eyes.

As it drew nearer, the crowd on deck began to shout, "Help. Save us!" One of the crew members climbed on top of the engine room and waved a piece of white sail.

"Uncle Hiep, what's that?" Mai said.

"An oil tanker." He held his hand to his forehead to shield his eyes from the sun. "They won't stop for us."

"They have to stop. Why wouldn't they?" said Mai, pushing through the crowd at the rail to get a better view.

The tanker chugged toward them. About ten yards away, it stopped and a man threw a heavy line toward their boat. One of the crew members caught it, tied it to their prow, and the tanker began to cut through the sea with their trawler bobbing along behind. The waves sloshed across the deck, soaking Mai, who stood grasping the railing, her feet spread to maintain her balance.

"Land, land."

A blur of mountains and green bordered by a thin strip of sand hovered over the ship's rail. The oil tanker left them drifting within sight of a small island.

"We're going to make it," Hiep said. Fresh air filled her lungs. Slowly the strong current washed their trawler towards the island, scuttling it on the coral reefs.

"We can't go any closer. You'll have to swim," the captain said. One by one the refugees plunged into the shallow sea.

"Come on, Mai," Hiep said, grabbing her hand.

"No, I can't," she said. "I'm afraid."

"Just hold onto me," he said.

Together they climbed over the rail and plunged into the water, fingers intertwined. The sea's surface hit her body with a harsh blow, knocking the breath out of her. Salt water stung her eyes and nostrils and filled her mouth as she sank deep below the surface. Her chest felt as if it would burst. *Where is Uncle Hiep?* She thrashed her arms and legs and came up sputtering, yelling for help. Just then he grabbed her arm and pulled her through the water until her feet touched the bottom and they were able to struggle up the beach, scraping their feet on the sharp coral.

"We made it," he panted, sinking into the sand, his black hair plastered against his head.

Mai looked up and saw towering palm trees laden with coconuts and rows of brown cloth held up by tent poles silhouetted against the twilight sky. Hammocks hung three-deep were suspended between the poles. Vietnamese women hunched over smoky cooking fires while barelegged children played in the sand. A large structure open on all sides, with a shiny tin roof held up by wooden beams, stood in the center. A sign in front had a large red cross on it and words she couldn't read.

The people on the island swarmed around them as they stumbled across the sand, calling out a chorus of names: "Chin, Phuong, Hien." Then they recognized their own.

"Mai, Hiep," a shrill voice shouted. Thin hands with long ragged fingernails pulled Mai out of the throng and bare arms smothered her in a hard embrace. When Mai managed to pull away, she saw a short bony woman with a broad face, fat lips, and wide-set eyes, her dark hair pulled back behind her ears. Small Auntie, her mother's sister-in-law, smiled at her.

"I can't believe it. You poor child. Don't worry. I'll take care of you." She bowed to Hiep and pulled them after her. "Come, you have to register."

She led them to the large building where, along with everyone else from the boat, they gave their names to several young men with clipboards who told them to report back the next morning for processing.

"You come live with me. Our boat's down on the beach. You can't get living space for two."

Mai wasn't sure where she was or what was happening. She only knew that somehow she'd landed on this island and that Small Auntie was going to take care of them. Mai remembered Small Auntie visiting them to celebrate Tet, the Vietnamese New Year. And a couple of times Mother had taken her to visit Small Auntie. It had been a long time since she had seen her. She tried to remember, but remembering could wait. She was just grateful that they were with family. Now Mai followed Hiep and Small Auntie down the beach.

Along the way, Small Auntie told them that she and Uncle Sang had been on the island for a year.

"It took us eight days to get here. We ran out of food and water, and the Thai pirates attacked us and took all our gold. They killed three of the men who resisted them trying to protect the women." She stopped talking and shuddered. Then she swept her arms through the air and said, as if she were giving a tour, "This island is called Pulau Tengah. It belongs to Malaysia. The United Nations." She stopped and looked at Mai and Hiep to make sure they were listening. "They're good. Set up this camp. The Red Cross. They work with them. Food. Medicine. They can find people for you. The Vietnamese workers, they're okay. Watch out for the Malaysians soldiers. Bad. They don't want us here."

She and her husband, their four children, and her brother and his wife were living in the fishing boat that had brought them to the island. Because Sang had been the engineer on the boat, the owner had let them keep it, beached on the shore, while he stayed on the north end of the island in his own tent with the wealthy refugees.

"A very rich man," Small Auntie exclaimed, "but he's very good to us."

When they arrived at Small Auntie's home, Mai saw a wooden fishing boat, about half the size of the trawler they'd arrived on, tilted in the sand, the paint on its sides chipping away. Small Auntie handed each of them a bowl of rice. Mai could not eat it, but she swallowed a few sips of water.

"Come, you need to get clean," Small Auntie said, picking up two metal buckets filled with water. "Here, you carry this," she said, handing one to Uncle Hiep and leading them back to a row of aluminum shower stalls that edged a deep thicket of palms. She pointed him to the men's stalls and handed Mai a bucket of water.

Mai stepped into the shower stall and poured the water over her salty, vomit-soaked body. Never had a bath felt so good. Small Auntie entered, rolled up the sleeves of her loose blouse, and scrubbed her back so hard Mai thought the skin was going to come off. But she bit her lip and said nothing.

Later, Small Auntie led her back to the boat and pointed to a space on the deck next to her four children who were sound asleep, their bodies curled toward each other like puppies.

"You can sleep here. My husband will be back later. My brother and his wife too. Do you remember them? They came with us to your house for New Year's once."

"Of course, Auntie," answered Mai, though she did not remember.

Mai sank to the hard deck, stretched out her legs, and felt her tight muscles pull in pain. Ah. Finally, to have a place to sleep. Surrounded by family, where someone wanted her. She could smell the sweet sweat of the children's bodies, hear their gentle breaths, along with the loud snores whistling from Hiep asleep flat on his back. Her stomach churned as if it were still at sea. What now? She touched the gold bracelets in the waistband of her pants. Mother had been right. They had brought good fortune.

Three

"Mai, are you awake?" Hiep's voice floated over to her, interrupting her dreams. Mai started to move and felt the hard surface beneath her. Of course, she remembered now. They were with Small Auntie and her family.

"Mai, wake up." An insistent tug on her shoulder.

"Uncle Hiep, is that you? I couldn't remember where I was."

"You were moaning last night."

"I had some bad dreams," she said, still shaking. "I could sleep all day." She yawned.

"We can't do that. We've got to go back to the registry."

"Oh, please, just a little longer…"

Hiep nudged her with his foot. "Get up, you lazy girl."

Mai sat and peered up at Hiep frowning down on her. Where was Small Auntie? And the children? The boat was deserted, though wisps of smoke came from a cooking fire nearby. Above her, pale purple and pink threads of light painted the eastern sky, erasing the night. Beyond her, she could see the gray-blue sea, their abandoned fishing trawler, forlorn, caught on the coral reefs.

She jumped down from the boat to the sand and followed Hiep past the light brown tents sprinkled along the beach to the Red Cross tent. Inside, a long line of men, women, and children waited to be interviewed. Mai sat on the ground at Hiep's feet while he filled out a form that a young Vietnamese man had handed him. She looked at the tables, where man sat interviewing refugees. The old woman who had been next to her on the boat was ahead of them, leaning on her son's arm. Hiep finished filling out the form and handed it back to the young man, who carried it over to a table where a man speaking English sat with a Vietnamese translator next to him.

Mai remembered the American soldiers on the Mekong before Saigon had fallen. One had given her a chocolate bar. So delicious. She should have shared it, but instead she had taken it to her room and eaten it all. Perhaps this man was an American. He finished interviewing the couple sitting at the table and called their names.

Mai pushed her hair out of her eyes. Hiep grabbed her hand and they went over to the table. She prayed that they would give the right answers so that they could go to America. Hiep gave his name and age first, and then Mai was asked for hers.

"Nguyen Mai" she said in the traditional Chinese way, last name first. "I'm fourteen." She knew that if she'd said she was younger, she would get to go to school longer in America. But Mother and Father had taught her to always tell the truth, and so she did. Hiep gave his brother's name and address in the United States, in that strange place called

Chicago. When the Red Cross made contact with Third Uncle, Hiep would ask his brother to sponsor them.

"We'll do everything we can," the young man said through the translator, his forehead beaded with perspiration, his face bright red with the heat. "Sometimes it takes a while. And, of course, there are so many waiting to leave. Just listen for your name to be called on the loudspeaker; that's how you'll know a decision has been made." Then the man gave them their meal tickets.

Mai left the Red Cross building with Hiep feeling confused.

"How long will it be?" she wanted to know. The uncertainty scared her. Would they be here a month? A year?

"I don't know, Mai. But we have a much better chance because we have family in America. I'll hang around the Red Cross in the mornings and listen for our names to be called." Hiep's voice wavered and he dug his hands into his pockets. Mai could tell he was frightened too.

As they walked back to the boat, Hiep asked Mai for one of her gold bracelets to pay Small Auntie for their living space. Small Auntie had asked him for money as she had led them to her boat.

"Mother told me to keep these. They'll bring us good fortune."

"Mai, this is our good fortune." Hiep held out his hand.

Mai reached inside her pants, ripped part of the seam, and slid a gold bracelet out. She slipped it onto her wrist. So beautiful. Then she slipped it off and handed it to Hiep.

"Here, take it. I still have one left. Don't ask me for that.

And don't tell Small Auntie I have it. She'll want it too." No wonder Small Auntie had grabbed them on the beach. *Don't trust anyone,* Father had warned them.

Hiep took the bracelet and put it in his pocket. "You're right. I think she hopes we have a lot of gold, but we're lucky to have a place to live. Two people alone aren't assigned a living place."

Mai believed what he said was true, but she'd promised Mother. She hoped she would understand. One bracelet would still bring them good fortune. She would never give that away.

Hiep walked away and Mai squatted in the sand and watched the waves cascading onto the beach. Where was she? Where was the world she'd lived in before that day three years ago, in 1975, when the Communists had taken over her land? Before then, life had had a predictable rhythm. She'd never worried about going hungry when she saw the sacks of rice coming to her family's rice mills to be processed.

How she loved her ancestral home. If she closed her eyes and tried, she could see the entertaining room, the family altar in the front. Grandfather sat in a carved chair with a high back, sipping tea, smoking his big cigars, and visiting with the village elders. Mai could still smell the aroma of his cigar smoke and hear his voice above the others as they discussed the rice crop.

Beyond that was her grandparents' bedroom, with an elaborately carved wooden bed draped with mosquito netting and covered with a thin mattress. Her own bed was a straw mat on a wooden bench that she'd shared with Ba Du, her nanny, until she'd turned five and her mother thought she was old enough to sleep alone.

She thought about Father, so sure of himself. He had managed all the rice mills for Grandfather. But later, when he'd sat under the mango trees and talked with her uncles, his voice was fearful and his eyes had dark circles under them.

She rose from the sand and walked toward the boat where Small Auntie was beginning the evening meal.

"You're lucky they let you ashore," Small Auntie said as she squatted on her heels and stirred the rice over the open cooking fire outside the boat. "So many people here."

Hiep handed Small Auntie the gold bracelet. She shook her head, turned it over in her hands to examine it, and then tucked it into the pocket of her shirt.

"Too many. When we first came a year ago, the island was almost deserted. Now the soldiers only let you land if your engine is broken. So many people suffer." She sighed and stood up, wiping her hands on her long loose pants. "If the soldiers find out that your engine does work, they will tow you back out to sea, to face the Thai pirates who rob and rape. If they don't get you, thirst and starvation will."

"Why would the soldiers do that?"

"Too many people here. Island's too small."

"But what do the people do?"

"I don't know." Small Auntie shrugged. "There are other islands. Sometimes a storm comes and they drown. When I came, we almost didn't make it. But my husband, he's a smart man. He kept the engine running. We would have all died, all two hundred of us."

Small Auntie looked up at Mai, who widened her eyes in disbelief. Two hundred on this small boat? Three hundred people had been on her boat, but it had been much bigger than this one.

Mai thought of the rest of her family. What if they were out there in a boat, drifting with no food or water as she had been, and no one rescued them?

"Enough of this." Small Auntie smiled. "You're here, and you must help. You can start by watching the children while I finish the cooking. They are always getting too near the fire."

She pointed to the four small children playing in the sand. The oldest was Minh, a boy about ten, holding a ball of string that he tossed in the air. Two little girls, Huong and Diep, who appeared to be about six and four, sat quietly and watched him. The youngest girl, Nhu, toddled toward Mai with her arms outstretched. Mai bent over and picked her up, surprised at how light she was. The child smiled and reached out for her hair. Mai sat down next to the other children. "Want to play a game?" she asked.

They didn't answer, their solemn eyes fixed on her. She showed them a game she had played with her sister Tuyet. She drew some squares in the sand and threw a pebble on the first square and hopped to it. Then she threw the pebble to the second square. "Here, you try."

They watched her silently, slowly joining in. She was happy they were entertained, but a sad feeling came over her. She missed her family.

Small Auntie interrupted her thoughts. "Tomorrow morning, Mai, go to the Red Cross headquarters with Minh and get our food. The ship comes about eight. Get there early before they run out."

Small Auntie gathered the rice bowls and called them over to eat. She smiled as Mai helped the children before serving herself.

Mai felt safe with Small Auntie. Even though she was a small woman, about Mai's height, she could hold a crying child on her hip with one arm and lift a cooking pot full of rice with the other. Her voice was strong and full of authority. Uncle Sang was off at the wells. Fresh drinking water was scarce and the men spent their time digging while the women and children lined up three times a day for food rations, hauled water, and gathered twigs for the cooking fire.

"Digging wells is dangerous work," Sang warned them that evening around the fire. "Not many tools. Sometimes I have to work with my bare hands. Scoop the sand into buckets and dump it on the ground." He dug his hands in the sand and let it run through his fingers. "Men have died," he said, lowering his voice. "Cave-ins. Thirty meters down—very deep. You be careful," he said, pointing to Hiep. "Tomorrow you will leave with me in the morning for the wells." He stood up and stretched. "Now I must rest." Sang turned and disappeared into the evening shadows.

Mai was worried, but Hiep was excited. He strutted around, proud to be considered a man even though his hands, Mai noticed, were soft, those of a student, not a laborer. *Great-grandfather, be with him,* she prayed.

Four

The next morning, Small Auntie shook Mai's arm. "Wake up, Mai."

Minh, short and wiry with black bangs that hid his dark mischievous eyes, clambered out of the boat behind her and together they went to collect the food, Mai stumbling along with her eyes half-open. The sand was cool beneath her feet and the tang of the salty sea air revived her.

She could see a line of young girls and boys starting to form at the ocean's edge. Red Cross workers stood behind tables piled high with boxes of food. She twisted her long black hair around her fingers, hoping she wouldn't disappoint Small Auntie. What if they ran out of food before it was her turn? She felt the food tickets that she and Hiep had been issued when they arrived. Minh carried the tickets for the rest of the family.

"Don't ever lose these," Small Auntie warned.

Small drops of perspiration gathered above Mai's parched lips. She closed her eyes to dispel the hunger that was rising in her stomach. A young man pushed forward, bumping her. At last it was her turn. The man at the table spoke in a language she did not understand, his gold tooth flashing in the sun. He repeated what he'd said and frowned at her. When she pulled her food tickets from her pocket and held them out, he shoved two long rolls at her.

Minh spoke to the man in his language, and he smiled and gave Minh his ration and an extra roll. Why had he done that? Mai wanted an extra roll too. One roll was not enough to quiet the angry roar coming from deep within her.

"What did you say to him, Minh?" Mai demanded, the hot sand stinging her toes as they walked away.

"I said, 'You do a good job.' He liked that."

"But what language was that? I didn't understand it."

"Cantonese. He's from Saigon."

"How did you learn it?"

"I traveled there many times with my father. I just picked up a few phrases. I'll teach you," he offered.

"I'd like that," Mai said, deciding that she might grow to like Minh.

Mai and Minh crawled up the side of their beached boat home. Minh handed his rolls to Small Auntie, and Mai and Hiep sat down to eat theirs. As Mai bit into hers, a sweet custard spurted out the end. She licked it off her fingers and took another bite. The custard hiding in the center of the roll spilled out into her mouth.

"Eat slowly, Mai. Your stomach is not used to such rich food," Hiep warned.

"Mai, Minh," Small Auntie called. "When you finish, take the children. The wood pile." She pointed to a few twigs in the corner. Small Auntie sat on the deck of the boat suckling Nhu, who sighed contentedly.

Huong and Diep tagged behind Mai and Minh as they crossed the sand to the edge of the jungle, searching for wood for the cooking fire. They passed groups of men cutting down trees for tent poles. Mai had never gathered wood before; her father had hired servants for that. She missed her father and her home. She cried as she stumbled on a branch in the path and fell to the ground. Minh heard her cry and doubled back.

"All right?" he asked.

"I'm fine," she said, ignoring his outstretched hand as she pulled herself up. She didn't want him to think she was helpless.

"Where are your parents?" Minh asked.

"They couldn't come. They're back in Vietnam."

"I'm glad my parents came with me. I would have been afraid without them."

"I was afraid."

"You're brave."

"No, they made me leave, but they'll be coming. They promised."

"I like it here," Minh said. "Lots of kids to play with. No school. You'll see. You'll like it too."

"No school," Mai said. "I miss going to school." She remembered how when they were in hiding, Mother had tried to give them lessons but was exhausted from working in Ông Ngoai's factory. Father, tired of hearing Mai's complaining, had sent her to a tutor, but it was expensive and dangerous to be seen out in public. Someone might report them. And then they would be taken to prison or even worse. So he'd stopped.

Would she ever get an education? She didn't want to

be like the farm girls who spent their lives working in the rice paddies, bending over all day, burdened by a baby on their backs, endlessly planting rice, their skin dark from the sun. Or like the factory workers trapped inside all day. No, she was going to be somebody important.

"I don't miss it," Minh answered. "Too much work."

They walked on, searching the jungle floor for firewood. Much of it was bare. Small Auntie had told them that over four thousand refugees lived on this once-deserted island, and that more came every day, clambering dazed from crowded boats as she had. Families lived side-by-side under brown tarps where the beach met the edge of the jungle, away from the ocean's tide, sleeping in rice bag hammocks hung three-deep between tent poles, cooking over fires built with rocks in the sand, waiting, waiting in a world where privacy no longer existed and today was the same as yesterday.

Mai could smell the stench of the fouled water along the shore where makeshift toilets had been built on narrow platforms out over the ocean. She stepped around one of the piles of tin cans and garbage littering the sand. Their boat was in Trung Dao, the central beach where the UN and the Red Cross had their processing tents and the supply ship came.

"The rich refugees live down there," Minh told her as they walked, pointing down the beach to the north end of the island. "It's called Bac Dao. They have so much money they hire the Malaysians to work for them. And there's the market."

Mai could see men and women sitting in the sand with their goods spread out before them. "Have you ever shopped there?" she asked.

"Oh, Mother goes there a lot. Sometimes we save our food and trade for clothing or whatever we need."

"Who lives down there?" Mai asked, pointing to the other end of the island.

"That's where a lot of the single people live. We call it Nam Dao, or the southern beach. I've never been there. It's hard to get to. No one lives on the other side of the island. Too many mountains and rocks."

Mai bent over and picked up more twigs. The girls followed her and when they had each gathered an armful, they turned around and followed Minh back to the boat. Small Auntie smiled as she saw them approach.

"Put them over here." She pointed to the cook fire, a hole dug in the sand and surrounded by three rocks. "Tonight we will take in what we don't use. Thieves."

After a drink of cool water, Mai and Minh walked back to the shore to line up for the food rations for the noon meal. Minh coached Mai on her Cantonese as they approached the lines waiting for the ship's return. For this meal, Mai received a cup of rice, a can of sardines, and a can of vegetables to be shared with Hiep. In the evening Mai and Minh would collect a can of meat, a can of vegetables, and a cup of rice for each person.

On the Mekong Delta, she could catch a fish in the river or pluck a mango from a tree anytime she wanted. She had never seen food in a can before. What a strange idea. She smiled at the short man with the gold tooth. Then she carefully spoke a phrase in Cantonese that she and Minh had practiced.

"I am very hungry today, honorable one. Could you spare some extra food?" She showed him her ticket.

He smiled back and handed her an extra can of peas. She hugged them to her chest and hurried over to Minh, who was dropping the rest of their food in a torn cloth bag.

"It worked."

"You were good," he said, "but don't let anyone know."

"I won't. Why would I do that?" She hated to be chastised by him, a boy four years younger, but she dropped her voice and peered behind her, hoping no one was looking.

"Tonight I'll teach you another phrase. This is fun. He thinks we're Cantonese."

"What happens if he finds out?"

"Don't worry. You picked up the accent."

The lines of children waiting their turn for food paid her no heed, busy laughing and talking as they whiled away the time. A few younger children sashayed through the waves at the edge of the beach.

Small Auntie handed her a bag of clothes when she returned. "Eat, and then take these and wash them in the ocean."

Mai filled her bowl with rice, peas, and a few sardines. She tried to eat slowly, savoring each bite. Invigorated, she dragged the bag to the ocean's edge and stepped into the swirling waves. She had never washed clothes before. She pulled a pair of children's pants out and dipped it in the ocean. A wave came and the bag of clothes started to float out to sea. She ran to grab it, dropping the pants. She dragged the bag back to shore and stumbled into the water again, but it was getting deeper and the pants were floating away from her. Then suddenly they started floating back to her as the waves returned to the shore.

The ocean wasn't like the river she had played by. This water was different—salty and with a strong current that could sweep you out to sea if you weren't careful. She pulled the pants from the waves and knelt down and scrubbed them.

When she finished washing all the clothes, her raw knuckles stung from the salt water. The bag with the wet clothes in was twice as heavy as before. She trudged back to the boat grasping it in both arms, then rinsed the clothes again in a bucket of fresh water and laid them out to dry on the bow of the boat.

Small Auntie walked over to inspect them. She held one of the T-shirts up in both hands.

"You need to scrub harder, Mai. Look, this is still dirty. Haven't you ever washed clothes before?" She balled up the shirt and carried it to the boat. "You can wash this again, tomorrow."

"Yes, Small Auntie." Mai bowed, her eyes cast down, but inside she was not bowing. She had worked hard, but Small Auntie did not care. Tomorrow she would show her. That shirt would shine.

The children clamored around her to play, Nhu sitting on her lap while Huong and Diep sat on each side. She put her arms around them, comforted by their warm bodies. Minh came in from gathering wood.

"Oh, there you are," he said. "I was wondering where you were." He pulled his string ball out of his pocket and started tossing it in the air. One of the girls grabbed it from him.

"Give it back," Minh laughed, and she tossed it in the air.

"I was washing clothes."

"Want to play ball?"

"I'm tired. Sit with us." Mai pointed to the spot beside her.

"Here, let's draw in the sand." Minh knelt down and drew a boat in the sand with a stick. Mai watched him, and then traced a picture of a house with her index finger.

"What's that?" Minh asked.

"My house, the one I used to live in."

"I remember visiting your house. It was very big. Your family is very rich, aren't they?"

"Not any more, Minh. Who told you that?"

Minh hesitated. "My mother. She said your father was the richest man in the village and that you brought a lot of money out with you."

"That's not true, Minh. The Communists took everything. We were lucky to leave with the clothes we were wearing." Mai stared at him. "I remember you now. You were very small. You used to cry at the fireworks."

Minh's face turned red. He still was afraid of loud noises.

The thought of Tet, of the scent of the yellow *mai* blossoms decorating their house, of the soft feel of her *áo dai*—the pale pink silk dress with the flowing pants underneath that Mother had the tailor sew for her—made Mai homesick. Before the war, Tet had been the most fun. Mai could feel the excitement just thinking about it. It was the only time her father stayed home and even *he* helped clean the house.

Mai pictured her aunts, parading through the doorway

hung with the beautiful *mai* blossoms and proudly presenting their best dishes: chicken, duck, and pork. Nine dishes would be spread on the dinner table; nine for luck, at the biggest meal of the year. Soon there would be lucky red envelopes with money in them for each of the children and fireworks exploding in the night sky. The whole family together, aunts and uncles, cousins, and grandparents, celebrating the beginning of a new year. All the shops were closed and not even the poorest person begged, for if you begged on New Year's Day, you would be fated to beg the rest of the year. That's what Father had taught them.

The war had not stopped Tet. They still celebrated, but the aunts did not come, the fireworks did not explode, and there were fewer red envelopes for Mai to tuck in her pocket. Gone were the large platters of food. She was lucky to get some rice to eat. Mai longed for the day when the war would be over and they could all be together again.

"Mai, help us." Minh had moved down to the water's edge with the girls and was scooping up the wet sand, packing it in piles. The girls helped him dig while Nhu waddled over and sat down in the water-filled hole. If Mai closed her eyes, she could pretend she was at home in her family's garden, surrounded by her brothers and sisters.

"Get her out of here," one of the girls complained.

Mai opened her eyes and gently lifted Nhu out of the way. "Here, you can play over here."

"You know, Mai, when I first saw you, I didn't think I'd like you," Minh confessed.

"Oh, why?"

"You seemed angry. I didn't think you liked me."

"I am angry, but not with you. I hate it here. All I want to do is get out."

"But we're safe and we've got food. Isn't that enough?"

"How can you stand being a beggar? I'm glad Father can't see me now. He would be so ashamed."

"Well, Mai, we've got to eat. And unless you've got a better idea, we'd better get down to the shore and stand in line. Hey, today's Thursday. Do you think it will be fish or chicken? And fresh vegetables. Let's get there early. Maybe they'll have bok choy."

Mai brightened. Fresh food would be a treat after the canned food and rice. She and Minh scampered to the shore and joined the line, crowding the tables, all hoping to be first.

A woman in front of her shouted, "Stop him. He took my rice."

Mai turned and saw a white-haired man, his body bent, clutching a bag. A young woman with a toddler at her side was pointing at him. The man started to run, but tripped in the sand and a soldier hit him in the face with his rifle butt. He started bleeding from his mouth. Three teeth lay in front of him as he struggled to get up. The soldier turned away. The woman bent over and picked up her rice.

Mai looked at the old man, who was holding his hands to his bloody face, with a mixture of pity and anger. Walking over to him, she stretched out her hand. He grabbed it and stood up. No one else came near. He shuffled away, clutching his jaw.

She had worried about someone stealing her food. There

wasn't always enough, but who would steal from a mother and a baby? How desperate must you be?

The soldiers marched around in their green camouflage uniforms toting guns and if you got in their way, they would kick you or hit you. Not even a dog in her father's house was treated so harshly. She was afraid of them, remembering the Communist soldiers and what they had done to her friends and family.

Five

Four months went by. Mai continued to collect the food with Minh, wash the clothes, watch the children, and fall asleep at night under the Malaysian sky dreaming of the day their names would be called over the loudspeaker and she and Hiep would go to America.

America? Would they have to work in the rice fields? How would she go to school? She hid these worries inside her the way she hid her gold bracelet from Small Auntie. At night she dreamed of her family. Each morning when she awoke, she thought she was at home until she remembered, and then sadness filled her.

She remembered pleading with Father not to send her.

"It's not possible. Your passage has been paid. The identification papers stamped. Now go to sleep. You'll have to get up early." Father had lit a cigarette and raised it to his lips.

There was no arguing with Father. Just do what he said. That night, she'd dreamed Father came to her with tears in his eyes and begged her forgiveness, assuring her they would never send her away. But the next morning, her mother had shown her the gold bracelets in the waistband of her pants before she stepped into them.

"Why must I wear all of these clothes? I'll be too warm," Mai had complained while her mother dressed her in three layers of clothing: three loose-fitting blouses and three pairs of pants.

"This is all you can take with you, Mai. You can wear the red blouse and black pants when you go to America. And," Mother reminded her, "don't tell anyone about the bracelets. They will bring you good fortune." She touched her forefinger to a lock of Mai's straight black hair dangling over her right eye and put her arms around her. Mai clung to her mother, feeling the softness of her body and smelling the odor of fish sauce on her breath, until her mother pulled her hands away. Mai would relive that goodbye embrace for a long time.

"You and Grandmother are going to take a *xe loi* to Father's cousin's house in Soc Trang near the mouth of the river. Just a shopping trip as usual. But you will stay there and wait for Hiep. He'll be along tomorrow."

I'll never see them again, Mai had thought, her throat raw. She'd rolled up her sleeping mat and put it in the corner of the small room where they all slept.

Since those terrible days in 1975, they'd hidden in Rai Rang with Ông Ngoai, at his textile mill just a few miles from their home. Because Ông Ngoai wasn't a wealthy landowner, the Communists had let him keep his factory. Mother and Father worked long hours stringing the looms and dyeing the thread. Mai could still smell the rotten egg odor from the vats of dye. She'd helped by watching Yen, the baby. Here, it seemed, they were safe. The workers wouldn't report them, but their world had shrunk and they had to be careful.

Yen, now a girl of four, ran over to Mai.

"Goodbye, Yen. Be a good girl."

Tuyet put her arm around Mai. "Goodbye and good luck. I'll see you in America," she whispered.

Quan, a skinny boy of ten, asked where she was going. "Just shopping with Grandmother," she'd replied.

"Come on, Mai, *xe loi's* here," Mother called as a motorcycle with a cab attached behind it pulled up. Grandmother, a tiny woman bent like a twig, her gray hair pulled back behind her ears, was waiting outside, her shopping bag over her arm. Mai could hear Father's teacup rattle when she walked to the door.

Mother thrust a red cloth bag at her. "Food for the journey," she said. Were those tears in her eyes, Mai wondered?

Mai and Grandmother climbed into the *xe loi*, which flew down the dirt road with the steady purr of its engine and the choking dust filling the air.

Mai remembered watching everything she loved disappearing: the alleys she'd played in with her brothers and sisters, Ông Ngoai's textile mill, its red tile roof gleaming in the sunshine, and most of all her beloved family.

A long time later, they entered Soc Trang. Grandmother had held Mai's hand while they made their way through a maze of alleys to the two-story brick house, where a sweet-faced woman with four small children clustered about her bowed and motioned for them to enter. She poured them each a cup of tea while her children stood in a row and stared with their small, dark eyes.

"Goodbye, Mai. Cousin will take good care of you. And

do what she tells you." Grandmother rose. She touched Mai's trembling hand.

"I will, Grandmother," she'd answered, in a voice so low she could barely hear herself

"Here," Cousin said. "Follow me." She padded down a dark hallway to a drab, windowless room. "Be very quiet. The neighbors." She nodded toward the outside wall, rolled her eyes, and put her finger to her lips.

Hiep had joined her the next afternoon.

Mai jumped up from her mat. "You've come. Why'd it take so long?"

"I had to leave later than I expected. Police around. Didn't want to arouse suspicion."

They left that night. When the house grew quiet and Mai thought she could not wait one more minute, a soft knock came at the door.

"Now," Cousin whispered, pointing down the hallway. Hiep and Mai slipped outside without speaking.

"Follow me," said Hiep, hugging the shadows.

Mai wiped her tears and stumbled after him until her legs throbbed with pain. They came to an inlet in the river. Above them, Mai saw the moon hanging like a gold medallion in the black satin sky.

A small wooden canal boat waited among the tall reeds. A young fisherman took Mai's hand as she stepped aboard. *Can we trust him?* A trembling couple with a small boy emerged from a bamboo grove and joined them. The boat sank low in the water with the six of them. The fisherman stood at the stern, and, moving two poles slowly through the water, pushed away from the riverbank. Mai could hear the rapid pounding of her heart against her chest wall, and the dip, dip, dip of the poles in the water as the current took them down the river.

Several hours later, the fisherman guided the boat behind a small island and stopped. The boat bobbed in the water. Half-awake, Mai leaned against Hiep's strong shoulder. Then the boat began crossing the river toward the old fishing trawler, with its long open deck and pilot house at the back.

Small boats appeared from all directions, headed toward the trawler like a swarm of bees to honey. When they reached the boat, a tattooed arm reached down and hoisted Hiep and her aboard. The captain, a one-legged man with a neat gray moustache, recognized them. Captain Le was a frequent visitor to their home; he was Father's cousin and a veteran of the South Vietnamese navy who had escaped execution by the Communists because of his war injury.

Mai hadn't seen Captain Le since they'd arrived on Pulau Tengah. She wondered what had happened to him. And she rarely saw Hiep anymore. He spent mornings at the Red Cross tent listening for their names to be called, then dug wells with Sang the rest of the day, and then disappeared after dinner.

One evening in early February, after she had helped Small Auntie wash the dishes, she and Hiep went for a walk along the beach. The sky was a black tent embroidered with silver sequins, the moon a sliver. The smoke of the cooking fires mingled with the salty sea air. Above her she could see the Silver River in the sky.

"I'm glad you stayed here tonight. Where do you go after dinner?" she asked Hiep.

"Oh, just hanging out with some of the guys I work with."

"I miss you."

"I'm just having fun, Mai." He stopped and stared at the sky.

"But it's not fun for me. I have to work all day for Small Auntie, and then in the evening, she still makes me tend to the children. Oh, Uncle Hiep, I want to go home. Why did we have to come here?"

"Now Mai, you know your father was right. We couldn't hide forever. They'd find us. And then they'd kill us or send us to the re-education camp. It couldn't stay like it was. You've got to be brave."

Mai walked along next to Hiep, feeling the soft sand on her feet. Oh, how she missed her family. She would try to be brave, but it wasn't going to be easy.

Six

The next morning, Mai was eating with Hiep by the fire. Small Auntie came around the side of the boat with her broom in her hand.

"Good morning," she said, smiling, her face smudged from smoke.

"Good morning, Small Auntie," Mai replied, standing up. Hiep rose too.

"Sit down, sit down. Eat your breakfast." Small Auntie stood in front of them and folded her arms.

"Is anything wrong, Small Auntie?" Hiep asked.

"I don't want to burden you with my troubles." Small Auntie sighed.

"Oh, tell us, please," said Mai.

"You've lived here for four months. Four months is a long time. You need to pay me more." She wiped her hand across her brow.

"We have nothing else to give you. We gave you the bracelet." Hiep's voice was firm.

"Oh, surely you brought more than one small bracelet. Maybe some diamonds?" Small Auntie smiled as if they shared a secret.

"We brought some, but pirates stole them," Hiep replied.

Mai sucked in her breath, shocked that Hiep would lie. There had been no diamonds. At least, none that she'd known about. Did Hiep have diamonds?

"Ah, such bad luck," clucked Small Auntie. "What about your brother in America?"

"We haven't heard from him yet," Hiep said.

Small Auntie stared at him with hollow eyes. "I have someone who wants to live with us who *can* pay. Perhaps you could find another place to live."

"Oh, Small Auntie, we are so happy here," Mai said.

"It makes me sad for you to leave, but if you can't pay, you'll have to leave tomorrow." She shook her broom and walked away.

"Uncle Hiep, what are we going to do? Small Auntie really wants us to leave."

"I heard her. I can't believe it. We're out of money except for your gold bracelet. We'll have to give it to her."

"No, we can't do that. I promised Mother. It's our good luck. We need to keep it. It will help us get to America."

"I don't know what we're going to do then."

"What was that about diamonds? Did you really bring diamonds?"

"Of course not, Mai. But I knew if I told her we hadn't left with anything, she wouldn't believe me."

"Where will we live? What will we do?" Mai started to sniffle.

"I have an idea. I know a group of single people who live down on the southern end of the island where I've been digging wells."

"But I don't want to leave here. Small Auntie is family. Surely she'll change her mind. Talk to her."

"Listen, Mai. The other night, I heard Small Auntie and Uncle Sang talking. They really do just want us for our gold. They think because our family owned a rice exporting company, we still have a lot of money."

"But you know that's not so. We've lost it all. But we'll get it back."

"Mai, we have no choice. We can live with my friends. I've met some girls there who are very nice."

"Oh, that's it. Do you have a girlfriend?" Mai often saw young couples walking together on the beach in the evening. Perhaps that was why Hiep was gone so much.

Hiep's face flushed. "I'll go talk to them tonight. I'm sure I can find us a place."

When Hiep returned to the boat that evening, the sun was down and the children were asleep. A haze of smoke hung over Small Auntie as she lingered by the fire, poking the embers. Hiep approached her while Mai hung back in the shadows, watching. She could hear them quietly talking. Then Small Auntie's voice got louder.

"It's impossible. You have to pay. I need money."

Hiep turned away and walked over to Mai. Small Auntie disappeared around the side of the boat.

"We'll leave in the morning. After breakfast. Like she said, she's already got someone to take our place. But we can go live with my friends. There is a place for us. Don't worry, Mai."

Mai gasped. How unfair. And she thought Small Auntie had wanted them because they were family. But Uncle Hiep was right. She had only wanted their gold.

Mai couldn't sleep that night. First her family had sent her away, and now Small Auntie. Didn't anyone want her? Sobs rose in her throat. She choked them down. She felt a heavy pressure on her chest, as if a huge hand were pushing her away. Tears dropped on the deck beneath her. She wasn't sure about Hiep's friends. She had only met one or two of them. Yet maybe it would be better there. Maybe she would see him more. Even though she would miss Minh and the girls, she would not miss Small Auntie chirping at her all day about her chores.

Mai wondered what her family was doing now. Were they still living at Ông Ngoai's, or were they somewhere in the South China Sea on their way to freedom? Maybe they would come to her island. Although she knew Father was out of money, perhaps he had been able to find free passage with one of his friends who owned a fishing boat.

Ông Ngoai had refused to leave Vietnam. He clung to the hope that the Communists would leave them alone. He said he had worked too hard for that textile mill. Mai had been happy living with him. A gentle man, he'd sat all day at the door of the mill in a bamboo chair listening to Chinese music on his record player while keeping an eye on his workers. Mai knew he must be lonely since Grandmother died. She laughed when she thought of him falling asleep after lunch, the brim of the funny plastic hat on his bald head tilted over his eyes, snoring to the sound of the music.

She remembered how angry her father had been about this. He had urged his father-in-law to put his money in a Swiss bank account and leave the country, but he wouldn't.

The waves banged at the shoreline. Daylight would arrive soon. She wiped her eyes and, exhausted, fell asleep.

When Mai awoke, she stared at the tarp above her. Sunlight blazed through a slit in it. She was alone. She could hear the mingled voices of children and adults outside on the beach. She had overslept. She stood up, slipped her bare feet into her dép, and gathered her few possessions—two blouses, two pairs of pants—which she placed in her red cloth bag. She felt the edge of her waistband for the gold bracelet. Ah, it was still there. Although she wore only a blouse and loose pants, it was hot. She peered down on the beach and saw Hiep standing by the cooking fire, eating a bowl of rice.

When she walked down to Hiep, Small Auntie rose from the cooking fire and smiled at her, but Mai did not smile back. Small Auntie's shoulders rose and she looked like a tiger waiting to pounce.

Mai picked up a bowl, scooped some rice into it, and stood silently, rolling the sticky rice into balls and eating them with her fingers, her eyes fixed on the ground. Small Auntie poured her a cup of water. Mai did not take it.

"We're going to miss you. Come back and visit. I hear the south end of the island is very nice. Not so crowded." Small Auntie rubbed her cheek.

Mai stared at her and at the girls playing in the sand. She did not want to go, but she would not let Small Auntie know that.

"We'll see you often, I'm sure. "

Mai bent over and quickly hugged each child. Minh was nowhere in sight. "Where's Minh?"

"Out looking for wood. I'll tell him you've gone."

Mai wanted to scream. She did not want to leave without saying goodbye to Minh. He would be angry that she had left, and she didn't want that.

"Please tell him I'll see him in the food line. Tonight." *Who will help me now? Uncle Hiep is busy digging wells.*

"Thank you for everything, Small Auntie. What would we have done without your kindness?" Hiep said as he gave her a ceremonial bow.

Mai knew that she should bow too. It would be disrespectful not to. After all, Small Auntie was her elder, and Mother and Father had taught her to respect her elders, but they had also taught her that no one should bring dishonor on the family name. She didn't bow.

"Small Auntie, I don't want to leave you. You are our family and we are all alone. Please let us stay." She reached out and touched Small Auntie's arm.

"Ah, Mai, if only that were possible. You see, life is different here." Small Auntie moved so that Mai's hand was no longer touching her arm. "It's too bad your family has not sent you money. I thought your uncle in America was very rich." Her crooked front teeth flashed as she forced a smile.

"Uncle Hiep told you we haven't heard from him yet. I've worked. I've done my share." Mai's voice rose.

"I have taken care of you these past months. You are a woman now. You and Hiep can take care of yourselves. I must take care of my family."

"But we are your family." How Mai hated to beg.

Small Auntie tapped her long nails on the cup of tea she

held in her hand. "I have four children, a husband, and a brother and sister-in-law. That is enough."

"I don't understand why you are treating us like this. You invited us to live with you. Did you only want our money?" Mai glared at Small Auntie. Father had told her it was a sign of weakness to show anger, but right now she didn't care.

"Foolish girl. War. Don't you know? We must take care of ourselves. Now go. When you have money, then come back." Small Auntie crossed her arms across her chest, her eyes hard.

Mai choked back a sob. She would never come back. She hated Small Auntie. No family loyalty. She was just like the Communists. She reached to pick up her small cloth bag and followed Hiep across the sand. When she looked back, she saw that Small Auntie had already begun sweeping the area around the boat with her stick broom.

"Mai, wait." Minh was running toward her. As he approached her, he dropped the bundle of wood he had been carrying. "Where are you going?" he called.

Mai turned around and looked at Minh. He was clad only in ripped shorts, dép on his dirt-caked feet.

"We're going to live with Hiep's friends, on the other end of the island."

"Take me with you," Minh pleaded.

Mai shook her head. "Your mother needs you." She tried to sound calm, even though inside she was shaking.

Hiep said nothing. Minh stamped his feet. "Why are you leaving? Don't you like it with us?"

"Uncle Hiep's friends want us to come," she lied. No use in Minh blaming his mother for their departure. Life was hard enough.

Minh grabbed Hiep's arm. "Don't go."

"I'll come and see you, don't worry," Mai murmured.

Hiep rolled his eyes and frowned at Mai as he removed Minh's hand from his arm and turned to leave. Mai hugged Minh and followed Hiep.

"Come back," Minh called, but Mai traipsed down the beach. She hoped she would like their new home. Minh would forgive her, she was sure.

Seven

Mai walked in Hiep's shadow down the hot sand beach, wading in the water's edge to cool her feet. As they rounded a bend, Hiep stopped. In front of them was the ocean, cutting a wide swath through the island and blocking their way. Mai froze. Hiep hadn't told her about this.

"What do we do now?" she called over the water's roar. A row of black slippery rocks formed a path across the water, but she knew she could never navigate it.

"Come on, it's easy. Just follow me. Hold my hand and we'll cross the rocks together. It's not that deep."

"I can't. I'll slip."

"Mai, you crossed an entire ocean. You can cross this. Here, hold on."

Mai knew she couldn't turn back now, not after the way she'd spoken to Small Auntie. She had no choice. Once again she was without a home, on her way to a new one, and once again she felt unwanted and pushed out. Tears gathered in her eyes and her whole being filled with a sadness she could not suppress. She just wanted to feel special to someone. Even Hiep had left her for his new friends.

He stepped out on one of the rocks and Mai grabbed his hand. She placed her foot on top of the first rock. Her toes gripped tightly into her dép. Hiep called to her to step to the next rock, but her legs wouldn't move. A wave came in and washed over her feet. She screamed.

"Come on, Mai, don't stand there."

Clinging tightly to Hiep's hand, Mai made it to the next rock.

"That's it. Come on, keep going," he coaxed.

Slowly she made her way across the swirling water, but just as she stepped to the last rock, Hiep's hand slipped out of hers and she started to fall, teetering on the edge until she found her balance and jumped to shore, where she sank down into the sand. Hiep stood, his head cocked to one side, his hands on his slim hips, chuckling.

"You did it. It's easy once you get used to it."

Mai didn't laugh. Tears spilled down her cheeks as she thought of Small Auntie and the humiliation of being asked to leave. Or was she crying because she was on an island somewhere in the middle of the sea, far away from her home and family, all alone, except for an uncle who was now laughing at her? She cried for the life in Vietnam that had been taken from her, for her childhood, for the unknown life awaiting her. And she cried because she'd stubbed her toe and it was bleeding. She'd had so many tears inside her. It felt good to let them out.

Hiep stopped laughing when he heard Mai's sobs.

"Mai, don't cry. You'll like it where we're going. Come on, get up."

Mai straightened her arm, bracing herself to stand. She wiped her sandy hands on her pants and brushed the hair out of her eyes. Hiep was the only one she would ever let see her cry. She would not cry again.

"I'll be all right. I just stubbed my toe."

Hiep led the way down to a palm tree-lined strip of beach surrounded on one side by towering mountains and on the other by clear blue water and coral reefs. A row of brown tarps suspended by tent poles ran like a ribbon through the white sand. A group of young women squatted around a cooking fire, talking, their voices muffled by the sound of the waves. As Hiep and Mai approached, one of the women rose and smiled at Hiep.

"You've come," she said, her eyes cast down, her black hair cascading over her face, a small black mole resting on one of her round, freckled cheeks. Her voice was soft and lilting, and reminded Mai of her sister Tuyet.

Hiep flushed with embarrassment, but, remembering his manners, he said, "Lan, this is my niece, Mai."

"We're so glad you're here. Follow me and I'll show you your hammocks." Lan folded her hands together and bowed. "This is our space. Six of us live here together and help each other."

Mai looked around and saw rice bag hammocks hanging between the tent poles.

"Those hammocks belong to my sister and me. Her name is Ngoc. And the other two belong to Kim and her brother, Tuan. You'll meet them all later. And these are for you. The Phams left yesterday for America."

Lan pointed to two hammocks in the corner. Mai was relieved to see that someone had sewn several rice bags together and draped them in front of the hammocks for privacy.

America. Mai felt her skin tingle. When would they get to go? Would there be a lot of food in America? Would she have friends? Whatever it was like, she knew that it had to be better than living under the Communists. Children spying on their parents, reporting their disloyalty. She could never have done that. In America, she would have a whole room of books to read and she could go to school every day. Maybe sleeping in the Phams' hammocks would bring them good luck. Perhaps they would be the next to leave.

Mai thanked Lan and reached up and placed her small bundle in the top hammock. "I'll take the top one since I'm smaller," she told Hiep.

He laughed. "Don't fall on me."

"Have you eaten?" Lan asked.

"Small Auntie fed us before we left," Hiep replied. "But I didn't want to eat with her."

Mai frowned at him. Even though Small Auntie had treated them badly, she didn't want to say anything against her. After all, she was family.

"Mai, you stay with Lan and she'll show you what to do. I have to get back to my job at the well. See you at dinner." Hiep smiled at Lan.

Mai stood silently and watched him walk up the beach. She worried about him at the wells, although he had assured her that he was very careful and took no chances. He was all she had here, and she did not want to lose him.

Water had become a big problem on the island. The ship from the mainland had to bring fresh water daily, but with more refugees landing every week, drinking water had been rationed to a half bucket a day for each person, collected in a precious bucket used also for washing dishes and clothes.

"How old are you, Mai?" Lan brushed a fly from her forehead.

"Fourteen."

"Just the age of my little sister. She left Vietnam with my mother and father after I left. I haven't seen her for a year."

"Do you miss her?"

"Oh, yes. I used to take care of her when my mother was working in the rice fields. She had the biggest smile, but I have my older sister, Ngoc, with me. You'll meet her later. You'll like her."

"I left all of my family too. Uncle Hiep and I came alone." Mai felt her chin quiver. "I can't even remember what they look like any more."

At night, lying on the deck of Small Auntie's boat, she'd tried to close her eyes and picture her mother and her father as they'd been the morning she left, but their features blurred like melted wax and the more she concentrated, the more distorted they became. Only Loc's face came through to her—sitting at the table that last night, his eyes bright with fever, as Mai learned that she would go in his place. Lucky Loc, at home with the whole family, while Mai was all alone. Did they think of her? Did they miss her as much as she missed them?

"Well, we'll be family now." Lan interrupted her thoughts. "Here, it's time to go line up for food. Come on."

Mai followed Lan out of the tent and back down the beach. Family. That's what Small Auntie had said at first, but she hadn't meant it. She would wait and get to know Lan before she trusted her.

Oh, no, Mai thought. She was going to have to cross the water again. Lan reached for her hand as they walked along, and Mai remembered walking with Tuyet, hand-in-hand down to their river. She was happy to have someone to walk with again like this. When they got to the rocks, Lan grasped her hand as they crossed and Mai felt a little braver.

She saw Minh when they got to the food lines. He was tracing letters in the sand with his toe. He did not look her way even when she called to him. She lined up with Lan and watched Minh collect his food and walk away, ignoring her. She would give him time. By tomorrow, maybe his anger would be gone.

Suddenly a woman came running down the beach, shouting. Small Auntie. She ran to Minh, crying. Then Minh was crying too. Mai wanted to rush over to them, but she stopped herself.

"Who's that?" Lan asked.

"That's Small Auntie and her son, who we were living with before."

Other people began gathering around them. Two soldiers guarding the food lines approached. At night the soldiers prowled around the encampment, beating people and stealing from them. Now they ordered the crowd back in line, while Small Auntie and Minh continued their crying.

"What happened?" Mai asked a teenage boy who'd returned to the line.

"Her husband was in an accident."

"What kind of an accident?"

"He was digging a well. It caved in."

"Is he all right?"

"I don't think so. They're trying to dig him out. They haven't found him yet."

Mai turned to Lan. "I have to go." Poor Minh. She had to talk to him.

"You go. I'll stay and get our food."

"Thanks." Mai handed her the food tickets and then approached Minh and Small Auntie, but they had started trotting down the beach. She had to run to catch up with them. "Minh, Small Auntie. Wait."

Small Auntie turned her head briefly but didn't slow down. Mai followed them to the path that led to Nam Dao, the end of the island where she now lived. She watched them cross the rocks, and then she followed. This time the water was down and the crossing was easier.

Down the beach, she saw a clearing at the edge of the jungle. Small Auntie pushed through the group of men surrounding the well and started to wail. Mai saw Hiep, down on his hands and knees in the sand with two other men, digging with a desperate determination.

"What happened?" Mai asked.

Next to her a gaunt young man, sweat beading on his bare chest, replied, "The sides caved in. We were down to thirty meters. Almost had water. Too bad." He shrugged and nodded toward the well. "He's not the first to die."

"Are you sure he's dead?" To have come so far across the ocean and to die like this was not fair, thought Mai.

"Well, if he isn't, he will be when they get him out. It's a long way down there." The man wiped his brow with the back of his hand and stared grim-faced at the well site.

Mai watched as Hiep and the men continued digging. She edged over toward Minh and put her arm around him. "They'll get him out, I know they will."

Minh looked at her with tear-pooled eyes and moved closer.

Hiep and the other men dug for several hours, their faces dripping, the sun blazing on their backs. They gulped water, but even then their hands kept moving as Small Auntie paced up and down on her short stubby legs, a glazed look in her eyes, encircled by family. Mai tried to approach her, but she wailed, continued her pacing, and would not be consoled. Mai picked up Nhu and held her in her arms. Nhu closed her arms around her neck and put her head on her shoulder, letting out a small whimper, a bewildered look on her little face.

When the sun stood high in the sky, Mai looked over at the well and saw Hiep and the other men standing up, brushing sand off their hands, slumping in despair. Small Auntie threw herself on the ground, wailing louder. Mai circled her arms around Minh's trembling shoulders, and then Nhu, distraught by the sight of her mother and brother crying, began to wail. Huong and Diep joined in the chorus, and the beach rang with their sounds of sorrow.

Mai was relieved that Hiep had not been the one buried in the well. She had not known Uncle Sang very well. He came and went, working late and returning to the boat in time to eat and go to sleep; he was a somber man who'd rarely spoken to her. She felt no pity for Small Auntie, whose wails were probably for herself and the hard life she would have without a husband. But Uncle Sang was a father, and now Minh and his sisters had no father. Mai knew how that felt.

She remembered the day the Communists had come and taken her father away.

Saigon had fallen, the Americans had left, and the soldiers had come to their village before her family had been able to go into hiding. Father, Grandfather, and her uncles had been sent to a re-education camp. She and her mother, along with the children, had been driven deep into the jungle and left to die. And they would have died if it hadn't been for a poor farmer who'd let them live in his barn and taught them how to fish and catch rain water for drinking.

She would never forget the morning almost six weeks later when she saw her father coming through the barn door. "*Cha*," she'd shouted, calling for him, running to him. He had rescued them, and that's when they'd gone into hiding at Ông Ngoại's textile mill. How happy she was that Grandfather and her uncles had been freed too, and that they would be coming to hide with them. A well-placed bribe to the authorities from Grandfather had been their salvation.

Small Auntie turned from the well. "It's your fault," she yelled, shaking her fist at Hiep. "He went down there and took your place. You are the one who should have died. What will I do without a husband? What will they do without a father?"

She sprang at Mai and grabbed Nhu from her arms. "And you, you ungrateful girl. I should never have taken you in. You brought bad luck to our family."

Mai's lips wouldn't move. Her brain blurred. Small Auntie's sister-in-law came between them and wrapped her arms around Small Auntie, pulling her away from Mai. Small Auntie struggled for a moment, but then, exhausted, allowed them to lead her away. Turning from the crowd, Mai ran down the beach in the opposite direction.

"Mai, wait. Wait for me." Hiep followed her, but Mai didn't stop running until she came to her tent. Hiep caught up with her as she sprawled in the sand, gasping. He knelt beside her.

"Why did she say that? She knows it's not true." Mai's eyes searched Hiep's face for an answer.

"She's angry with us for insulting her, and now she's grieving. She has to have someone to blame. It's not fair. " Hiep pounded the sand with his fists.

"But she knew the wells were dangerous." Mai cried.

"He volunteered. He's the most experienced, and the last part is the hardest. He made me come out when it got deep. No one wants to risk their life going after him." Hiep choked the words out between sobs.

Mai put her hand on his back to quiet him. Hiep raised his hands to his face and sat back on his heels.

"What will happen now?" She squinted at Hiep in the bright sun.

"About what?"

"The well," Mai answered.

Hiep stood up. "They'll close it. No one will want to go near it. It's haunted."

Mai shuddered. Would Sang's ghost come back to haunt

them? Father had told them that when a person died accidentally, his ghost would not be able to rest and would return to punish those responsible. She hoped Sang's ghost didn't think she and Hiep were to blame.

"Small Auntie? What'll we do about her? What if she tells everyone it's our fault?" Mai asked.

Hiep brushed the hair from his forehead and scowled. "No one will believe her."

"But we did live with her. And we were at the well. She's angry."

"Don't worry about her. We'll just stay away from her. She'll calm down. Let's get something to eat. I'm tired and hungry. Maybe Lan has cooked some rice and chicken."

Mai looked up at Hiep, whose face, once soft and boyish, had hardened into that of a man. She hadn't really looked at him closely until today, but now she saw her father in the way Hiep carried himself—chin up, looking straight ahead, unafraid. Could she be like that? She was her father's daughter. She knew that, and she was determined to survive, just as she'd promised.

Mai walked over to her tent and crawled into her rice bag hammock, her appetite gone. Oh, this bag was scratchy and made her skin itch. She squirmed to get comfortable as Small Auntie's words came back to her. Had they caused Small Auntie's bad luck?

She thought again of the way they had parted and was ashamed. She believed in luck. Hadn't the gold bracelet that Mother had given her brought them good luck? If there was good luck, then there must be bad luck too. But what caused it? Someone else could have died in the well today. Why had it been Minh's father? Had he brought his own bad luck, or did others bring it? Somehow, Mai thought, you must be able to control what happens to you. But right now she just felt lost and alone.

Eight

When it was nearing Mai's time to go to the well the next day, she thought of Uncle Sang and was afraid. *What if I fall in?* she thought to herself. The wells for drinking were much deeper than those for wash water. She had just cooked a bowl of rice for Hiep and herself, and they were sitting on the floor of the tent eating in silence when Lan slipped out of her hammock and came over to them.

"I heard what happened yesterday. Are you all right?" She leaned over and touched Mai's shoulders, but her eyes were focused on Hiep.

"I'm okay. It was a terrible accident." Hiep's voice faltered. "We couldn't get him out. It happened so quickly."

Lan nodded, her eyes warm and soft. "I heard you worked a long time. You did everything you could." She sat down beside them and crossed her thin legs.

Mai interrupted. "Small Auntie blames us. She says we brought her bad luck."

"But that's not true." Lan's voice tensed and her forehead wrinkled.

Hiep shrugged. "I know. But he did go down and take my place."

"Do you think Sang's ghost will come after us?" Mai put down her chopsticks.

Lan looked at her. "No, Mai."

"Are you sure? In our village, we heard tales of ghosts punishing people."

Lan shook her head and put her arm around Mai. "It's not your fault."

Her words did not reassure Mai, who pictured Small Auntie's hate-filled eyes as she shook her fist at them.

Hiep set his bowl on the ground and stood up. "I have to go. We're working on another well today."

"Be careful, Uncle," Mai said, putting down her chopsticks.

"Don't worry, little one. I'm always careful."

Mai watched as Hiep turned, walked out of the tent, and strode down the beach.

Lan turned to Mai. "I know he feels bad, but don't worry. I think Small Auntie just likes to talk."

Mai nodded, but she knew Small Auntie would not forgive them and that somehow she or Sang would punish them. She shivered, even though the heat of the day was already seeping into the tent.

A young man about Mai's age walked toward them, swinging two buckets and whistling.

"Kien, are you going for water?" Lan asked.

"Sure. Can I help you?"

"No, but you could help my friend Mai."

Mai blushed. How did Lan know that she was afraid to go to the well?

Kien turned toward Mai, his dark eyes smiling. "Of course. I'm glad to help."

Mai got her metal bucket and walked with Kien along the rocky beach, too shy to talk, but glad to have a distraction from her worries about Small Auntie.

"How long have you been here?" Kien broke the silence.

"About four months."

"I haven't seen you down here before. Where have you been?"

"We were living in a boat in Trung Dao, but we had to move."

"Look." Kien stopped and pointed to a small, black, worm-shaped creature among the rocks in one of the tide pools.

"What is it?"Mai asked as Kien bent over to pick it up.

"It's a sea cucumber. Here, want to hold it?" The sea cucumber wriggled in Kien's hand.

Mai shook her head.

"Ever eat one of these?"

"No." Mai wrinkled her nose. "Why would you want to?"

"Don't you ever get tired of canned food?" Kien asked.

"Of course, but I just wish for fresh fish like we had in Vietnam."

"Me too, but they're hard to catch. You have to go out in a boat, and we don't dare do that or the soldiers would never let us back on the island."

"What does it taste like?" Mai asked, her nose wrinkling.

"Sort of like squid. You have to clean them right or they

taste bad. Lan and some of the other girls at the camp know how to do it. They grill them or stir-fry them with some of our canned vegetables. I like them. After we get the water, let's come back and collect some for dinner tonight; then you can see if you like them." Kien dropped the creature back into the tide pool and watched it burrow down into the sand.

Mai gave a weak "okay," and she and Kien walked on down the beach to the well, where a line had formed to draw the daily water. A line for everything, thought Mai. How tired she was of standing in line. When it was their turn, Kien took her bucket, stepped to the edge of the well, and, grasping the rope tied to the handle, lowered the bucket until Mai heard a splash, and then he carefully drew it up. Kien lowered his own buckets and then he and Mai carried them away from the well and back to camp.

Mai glanced up at Kien as they walked along, grateful for his help, surprised at how easy it had been to talk to him. She'd never been friends with any boy outside of her family. Kien whistled as he walked along, his golden skin glistening in the sunlight, the muscles in his arms tight from the weight of the buckets. *It would be nice to have a friend like him, not a boyfriend, just a friend*, Mai thought.

When they got to camp, Kien set down his buckets and Mai put hers next to his, their arms bumping as they stood up. She jerked her arm away, embarrassed, but he seemed not to notice.

"Want to go catch sea cucumbers now?" he asked.

"I have to go line up for food. Could we do it in the morning?" Mai hoped Kien wouldn't think she didn't want to go.

"Sure, I have to go for food too. Let's go together."

Mai's heart sang. He liked her, but why? She'd always thought of herself as very plain, and she never knew what to say. Kien was quite handsome, with kind eyes that looked straight at you when he was talking, straight teeth that were as white as the sand, and an infectious smile that made her forget how alone she was. He seemed at ease with himself; something she had never felt.

They walked along, listening to the waves, watching the seagulls circling in the cloudless sky, breathing in the mingled smell of wet sand and sea air. When they came to the rocky inlet, she was relieved to have Kien's hand to grasp as they crossed.

"Where is your family, Kien?" Mai asked, looking up at him, glad that he was taller than her.

"I came by myself. Mother didn't have the money to come too."

"But what about your father?" Mai kicked the sand with her feet.

"My father was an American soldier. When he had to go, he wanted us to come with him, but my mother wouldn't leave my grandmother behind."

"An American soldier?" Mai looked at Kien again. Except for his blue eyes, he didn't look like an American. "What happened then?" She hoped he would not think she was prying.

"The Viet Cong came. My mother was afraid they would kill us if they knew we had an American connection, so she burned all the papers my father had given her to contact him." He shrugged his shoulders, and his head sagged.

"How will you find your father?"

"I don't know. If I can just get to America, maybe there will be a way."

"I have an uncle in America."

"You do?" Kien stopped and put his hands on his hips. "Have you heard from him?"

"No, but the Red Cross is contacting him." She wished she hadn't told him when she saw the pain on his face.

"I'm glad for you," Kien said. "I don't know where I'll end up. They say America needs lots of unskilled labor and that it's the easiest place to go. I hope that's true."

Ahead, they saw Hiep hurrying out of the Red Cross tent.

"We got a letter from Older Brother in America," he said, pulling an envelope out of his pocket. "He sent some money." He opened his fist and showed her a green bill with a *50* on it.

"We did! What did he say?" Mai wanted to see the letter herself, but she waited for Hiep's reply.

"Here, read it," he said.

Mai took the letter and held it in both hands as if it were a sacred scroll.

Dear Hiep, Younger Brother,

My wife and I are happy to hear that you and Mai have arrived safely at the refugee camp. We are filling out the papers to sponsor you, but you must know life here is very hard. The streets are not paved with gold. We have to work twelve hours a day seven days a week. We only have time to shop once a week. The weather in Chicago is not like Vietnam. It is winter

now and the temperature is 0 degrees C and there is
snow on the ground. Very cold.

Anh, Older Brother

Mai handed the letter back to Hiep, her eyes bright with excitement. "He's going to sponsor us. We're going to America."

For the first time since she'd left Vietnam, Mai's depression began to lift. Uncle and Auntie wanted them. They would have a home, and they weren't going to spend the rest of their lives on this island. Her dream of life in America was going to come true. But she did worry about the snow. The coldest she had ever been was in the spring on the Mekong when the winds blew. She had no warm clothes.

And the streets. Everyone had said they were paved with gold. What were they really made of? How did you eat if you couldn't go to the market every day? She hoped she would be able to go to school. Grandfather had big plans for her. He wanted her to be an international lawyer.

"It could take a long time, Mai. Remember, Small Auntie has been waiting a year now," Hiep said.

Small Auntie. She had forgotten about her. The joy she had felt turned to lead as she thought of Small Auntie's anger. She would not let Small Auntie take away her hope.

"But we have a sponsor. It won't take that long."

Hiep smiled and tucked the letter in his pocket. "I hope you're right." He turned to walk toward the well site. "I'll see you this evening. We'll write them a letter."

Mai smiled at Kien, who had been pretending not to

overhear their conversation. "It's all right. Did you hear? We got a letter from my uncle."

"That's great." Kien tried to sound enthusiastic, but his voice fell flat.

The two of them walked toward the Red Cross tent where streams of children milled around, some shouting as they kicked a string ball, others making little trails through the sand with pull toys made of tin cans and string as they waited for the food ship to come. A blond American girl wearing a white T-shirt with a red cross in the middle of it was teaching English to a small group of children seated at her feet.

"Do you know English, Kien?" Mai asked, for now that she was going to America she had to learn English so that she could study hard and go to law school.

"A little. The people in our camp are mostly students. They studied English at the university in Saigon. Sometimes they teach me words. They all want to go to America."

"I want to learn English. Is it hard?" Mai stopped where the young woman was teaching and listened. The teacher was holding up cards with letters and pictures on them, and the children were repeating them after her, in unison.

"A for apple, B for bear, C for cat ... "

"I don't think so." Kien answered, squinting at the cards.

Mai and Kien listened until it was time to line up for food. Mai tried to find the English teacher after they'd picked up their rations, but she was passing out food at one of the other tables. Maybe she could talk to her later, but after the distribution, the young woman left on the ship with the other American and European workers to go back to the mainland.

Mai had heard someone saying they lived in air-conditioned buildings there. She hoped the young woman would return in the morning, and then Mai would begin to learn English.

That evening, when the dishes had been washed and everyone was sitting around talking, Kien surprised her. Darkness surrounded them as the sun disappeared in the western sky, and Mai was thinking about crawling into her hammock and going to sleep when Kien appeared before the group carrying a guitar. Music. How Mai loved music! Lan, with several young men and women that Mai didn't know, got up to walk down to the beach.

"Come on, Mai and Hiep," Lan urged. "We're going to have some fun."

The full moon created a shimmering path across the ocean, making the water and the white sand as light as day. Mai sat down on the cool sand, looking at the others and thinking of her family. Was the same moon shining down on them?

Several others joined them, and then Kien picked up his guitar and started to strum some chords. His slim fingers plucked the strings and he started to sing in a soft alto voice. The strains of a popular Vietnamese song flowed from his guitar. The words were familiar to Mai, who joined in the chorus, singing, "*You asked me how much I love you, the brightness of the moon is a symbol of my love for you.*"

Other voices joined him and turned the beach into a magical world for Mai, a world where there was no war, no death, and no hunger. For a short time she could forget about Small Auntie. For a short time she was able to forget that she had no home. The young people around her were her family. The tent she lived in was her home. She belonged. And despite all the hardships, she felt a grain of hope.

She glanced at Kien, who was smiling at her, and she turned away, blushing. Hiep's face was aglow and his eyes had a faraway look. She saw Lan steal a glance at him and wondered if Lan felt the same way about Hiep that Mai felt about Kien. She had wanted Kien as a friend, but she was beginning to feel something more, something she couldn't describe. Was this what love was? She looked at the moon, full and bright, and knew it was the happiest time of her life.

The next morning, Mai carried her large plastic bucket and her small metal one to the washing well. She lowered the metal one several times, emptying it into the large plastic one. This would give her enough rinse water for her clothes and the dishes; the seawater was fine for washing, but her clothes needed a fresh water rinse or they would dry stiff, smelling of salt.

Later, at the drinking well, she saw Kien and blushed. He ambled over to her, his buckets clanging.

"Want some help?" He reached for her bucket. "I had to leave early this morning to get the sea cucumbers. I thought you would probably be tired after last night." He looked down at his feet, waiting.

"Oh, that's all right." She tried hard to pretend that she hadn't missed him. She didn't want him to think he couldn't go get them without her.

"We could go catch sea cucumbers early tomorrow morning if you'd like." Kien lowered Mai's bucket down the well. She heard the splash as it hit the water, and then Kien raised it slowly so that it wouldn't tip.

"I enjoyed the music last night. I didn't know you played guitar," Mai told him.

"It was my father's. He used to play it for my mother. When he left, he gave it to her as a remembrance." Kien's voice dropped and Mai regretted her question. She didn't want him to be sad because of her. His music had brought her so much happiness.

"But how did you learn to play it?"

"I taught myself. It's not hard. I could teach you."

Mai's eyes widened in surprise. "But that would take up so much of your time. I couldn't." No one had ever offered to help her like this.

"Yes, I insist. After dinner tonight. Let's take the water back now so we can go line up for food. Maybe that American girl will be back and you can learn some English."

The bucket had never felt as light as Mai walked alongside Kien back to their tent, where, after delivering the water, they began the long trek to the Red Cross tent in the center of the island. Kien extended his hand to her again when they approached the rocky crossing, but Mai shook her head. "No, I need to do this on my own," she said, and much to her surprise, she did. By this time the rays of the midmorning sun had turned the sand into hot coals, and they were forced to wade in the ocean to cool their scorched feet.

As they approached the middle of the island, the sparkling white sand lost its luster and faded into a dingy brown, contaminated by a swelling city of refugees. Mai stepped around a pile of discarded tin cans and thought about how beautiful and unspoiled her end of the island was.

When she and Kien arrived at the food tent, the American girl, Miss Cindy, was there, her blonde hair swept up in a ponytail, her sun-tanned arms holding up the letters of the alphabet, a throng of children at her feet. Mai edged over to the outside of the group and stared intently at the letters. They were very different from Chinese characters with their straight black lines, which she had learned to write at school; they were more round and flowing, like Vietnamese letters. Kien stood next to her and, together, they repeated the letters. If only she had something to write with so she could study them back at her tent.

She stood shyly watching the class until it was over. Then she approached the American teacher. "I would like to learn English, please," she said.

Miss Cindy smiled at her. "Everyone is welcome," she said in Vietnamese.

"Thank you. Can I come tomorrow?" Mai asked.

"Tomorrow after breakfast. Right here. What is your name?" Miss Cindy took out her notebook and pencil.

"Nguyen Mai," Mai whispered, her eyes lowered.

"Great," said the teacher. "See you tomorrow."

"Thank you, thank you," said Mai, clasping her hands and bowing. She was going to school again.

Mai thought of her school in Vietnam, the one Grandfather had built. How proud she was when he visited the school, arriving in his chauffeur-driven Cadillac, a distinguished-looking man dressed in a dark suit and tie, standing straight as a soldier as the students all marched in lines out of the school to greet him. She'd stood at attention with the others, her bobbed hair neatly combed, her white blouse tucked into her navy blue skirt. How she loved going to school and learning about anything, especially Chinese folktales.

Her favorite was the story of the two Trung sisters, heroines of Vietnam's rebellion from the Chinese a very long time ago. She loved the way they had led the nobles and captured many citadels and declared Vietnam's independence. She dreamed that one day she, too, would come back to Vietnam, charging in on an elephant, a saber in her hand, like the Trung sisters, the Communists running from her as the Chinese had retreated from them, her family bowing down to her in admiration.

A woman could change things. She could help her country, and some day she would. Women were not drops of rain, as the Chinese poet said, some falling purely by chance on luxurious palaces while other fell on muddy rice fields. This view was one her mother had taught her, but she didn't want to be like her mother, running to serve Grandmother's every whim, her life not her own, her children left in the care of a nanny. She would be like the Vietnamese women of old, warriors, judges, and traders. Women with power.

"It's time to go." Kien nudged her and she awoke from her daydream to the sight of her countrymen: old men with wispy beards; young mothers with hungry children clinging to them; once-proud men, their heads hanging in shame, waiting in line for their noon meal like beggars. Her eyes grew hard and she thought, *I'll never forgive the Communists for what they have done to us.* And she took her place in line.

Nine

The rhythm of the waves lapping the beach at nightfall failed to lull Mai to sleep as she lay curled in her hammock, a knot in her stomach. She closed her eyes. What was that? Something was moving near her. She opened her eyes. A figure floated toward her. It was Sang. But he was dead. She closed her eyes, praying he would disappear. But when she opened them again, he had moved closer. She could see his face now, twisted in agony. Sand poured from his mouth. His hands clawed the air.

"Help me. Help me," Sang screamed. "Don't leave me in this well." About him was the stench of decay and death.

Terrified, Mai hid under her blanket.

"You and your uncle will be punished," Sang's ghost called. And then he disappeared.

Mai couldn't move. If only Small Auntie had had a funeral for him, perhaps some chanted prayers to usher his spirit into the next world; that probably would have satisfied him. What did he want from her? She'd had no part in his death. With no body to cremate and no monks on the island to chant prayers for him, would Sang be forced to wander the four corners of the earth, weeping and wailing, looking for vengeance, unable to go into the next world? Grandfather had told her that this was what happened to people who died violent deaths and were not given a proper burial.

"Hiep, are you awake?" She peeked over the edge of her hammock at him, the moonlight seeping in underneath the brown plastic canopy that sheltered them and casting a silvery shadow on Hiep's closed lids. She watched his bare chest move up and down. He seemed to be sleeping, but how could he have slept with Sang's ghost in the tent?

"Uncle Hiep, wake up. I'm frightened."

Hiep opened his eyes and looked up at her. The ghost had disappeared, but the odor of decay remained.

"Mmm. What's the matter?"

"I had a bad dream, except it wasn't a dream. I was awake and Uncle Sang's ghost came to me. Can't you smell him?"

Hiep reached up and touched her hand. "Don't be afraid. Just a dream," he murmured, half asleep.

"Uncle Hiep, listen to me. We're in danger. He's after us." Mai grabbed Hiep's arm and shook it. Hiep opened his eyes again in annoyance.

"I can't sleep," she said. "Uncle Sang's ghost was here. He threatened us. Didn't you hear him?" Mai climbed down and crouched on the ground next to Hiep, who was stretched out in his hammock.

"Shh! You'll wake the others." Hiep rose, grasped Mai by the elbow, and guided her outside the tent, where a slight breeze sliced through the sultriness of the tropical night. "Mai, are you feeling all right? What did you eat today? Maybe it's upset you." He leaned close to Mai, and she could smell the odor of fish on his breath.

"Uncle, I'm not sick, and I'm not imagining this. Uncle Sang is out to get even with us. I think he blames you and me for his death."

"Mai, don't be foolish. Go back to sleep. We'll talk about this in the morning. Maybe I should go see Small Auntie." Hiep's voice softened as he brushed a tear from Mai's chin.

"What good will that do? You know how Small Auntie feels." Mai grabbed Hiep's hands and wouldn't let go.

"You don't believe those stories. She can't hurt us." Hiep removed Mai's hands from his and took a step away from her. "Sang is dead. Now come on and go back to sleep. I'm tired."

Mai knew she had made Hiep angry, but she was upset that he didn't believe her. Perhaps he was right. So much had happened to them since they'd left Vietnam she didn't know what she believed. She tiptoed back into the tent, careful not to disturb the others as she climbed back into her hammock, expecting to lie there sleepless until the morning light. She closed her eyes, afraid of the phantoms sleep might bring, and was relieved when the sun slipped into the tent and she heard Hiep call her name.

"Mai, I'm sorry about last night," he said, but Mai was not ready to forgive him, and she turned her back to him and pretended to be sleeping.

"Mai, wake up. Let's go see Small Auntie."

She peered at him through half-open eyelids but did not speak, knowing that her words would be useless.

"All right, I'll go myself. You stay here." Hiep strode out of the tent.

The words *don't go* stuck in her throat and a cold fear wrapped its icy tentacles around her.

She had avoided Small Auntie's boat yesterday as she'd lugged their tins of food back to the tent, cutting a wide swath around it. She'd seen a few curls of smoke from the cooking fire, a couple of holey T-shirts laid out to dry on some bushes, and a large oil can perched on a rock. Someone had propped Small Auntie's ragged broom against the peeling hull of her boat. A child's dép peeked through a mound of sand next to a tin can with a string threaded through a hole in its side. There'd been no sign of Small Auntie or the children. Mai was relieved not to see her, but she worried about the children. Where were they? Was Small Auntie too distraught to care for them?

Mai knew how grief could affect a person. Her cousin Trang, a year younger than she, had drowned in the Mekong while swimming with her three older brothers. Mai had been playing with two of her cousins under the banana trees behind their house. She heard a voice shouting for help, and only then did she look across to the path that ran by the Mekong and see a boy running and waving his arms.

"Trang," he gasped. "She fell in the river. We can't find her."

Mai had run inside for her grandfather, who alerted her father and Trang's parents, and they'd all rushed to the water where Trang's eldest brother was pointing to the spot he'd last seen her, but all they saw was the blue-gray water rushing by, its current swift and unforgiving.

Mai remembered standing on the shore with Trang's

parents and her own mother and father, watching as the rescue boat plied the water for Trang's body. She could still see the silhouettes of Trang's parents, bareheaded on the river's bank, standing in silence as they waited for some news of their daughter. Trang's three brothers stood in a row next to them, their heads bowed, their arms clasped behind them.

"You have all been warned about the river in the rainy season," Mai's father chided at dinner that night.

Mai's mother wept as she sat beside them. "Only seven. I hope they can find her. Poor girl."

"She might be caught in a deep hole. Who knows? This is what can happen if you do not obey your parents." Mai's father's face was stern as he spoke the words, but his eyes were misted.

The next afternoon when the unsuccessful search ended, Mai saw Trang's mother slap each of the brothers in the face. "You are no-goods," she cried, pounding the oldest son in the chest with her ball-like fists. "You do not watch your sister. Now she is gone forever and her spirit must wander."

The boys did not recoil. The nanny, a young girl of thirteen, stood by, trembling, her head bowed, her face covered by her hands.

"And you, your only job is to watch my daughter. Go, you are a disgrace. You bring bad luck. Leave the village and never show your face again." Trang's father's voice raged with grief and anger.

The nanny, cowering, crept away, carrying her small bag of belongings, her wide face smeared with tears.

Mai had come to know that anger was a part of grief,

and that someone had to be blamed. She was afraid for Hiep. Small Auntie would not absolve him of her husband's death, but would try to punish him, instead of intervening for him with her husband's ghost. Why had he gone to see her?

Sometimes Hiep could be so stubborn, like the time he'd insisted he knew the way to the zoo, refusing to ask for directions, and they had been lost for over an hour. She had sat quietly in the back seat of the car as he drove, with a cigarette butt between his fingers, one hand on the steering wheel, his other arm dangling out the window. After what seemed like all morning, the sun glaring on her through the side windows, the plastic seat covers sticking to the backs of her legs, he had turned to her and laughed.

"I think we're lost, Mai. Do you know where we are?"

Mai, her back stiff from sitting so long and her mouth dry as the paddies in winter, had answered him sharply. "Uncle, I don't know where we are. I'm only a kid. Ask someone for directions."

He arched his eyebrows in surprise at her retort, but he pulled over to the side of the road and stopped a young boy on a bicycle, asking him where the zoo was. She could see the boy, balancing a bundle of firewood on the back of his bicycle, point back down the road they had just travelled. Twenty minutes later, they parked at the zoo and Mai saw her first elephant, and when her new shoes hurt, her uncle had carried her piggyback. *Would she ever have such fun again?*

Mai hurried to get dressed and eat so she could go to English class. Though Hiep had not returned, she was not going to miss it waiting for him. The class had already begun when she arrived. Miss Cindy, the teacher, was writing some words on a chalkboard propped against a palm tree. A group of children and adults sat cross-legged on the ground in front of her. As she pointed to the words and pronounced them, the class chanted them after her. "Dog, cat, mother, father."

The list went on. Mai joined in, though the sounds were very different from Vietnamese. Then Miss Cindy wrote a phrase on the board.

"My name is Miss Cindy. What is yours?" she said. She pointed to Mai and smiled.

Am I supposed to speak?

The teacher nodded and waited.

Mai answered, "My...name...is Mai." *What's that next phrase? I can't remember.* She looked at Miss Cindy for help.

"Go on, Mai. Now ask your neighbor: 'What is your name?'"

Mai turned to the girl next to her. "What is your name?" she said, enunciating each word.

And so they went around the group, each person stating his name and then asking the next one what his name was. *This is fun*, thought Mai. English class flew by.

After an hour, Miss Cindy closed by teaching them a song. "Would you like to learn an American song? How many of you like baseball? Baseball is very popular in America. We sing this song at every game. It's called 'Take Me Out to the Ball Game.'"

Mai listened as Miss Cindy sang the song. She couldn't understand the words, but she liked their happy sound. Though she had never been to a baseball game, she hoped that when she got to America she would get to see one. She would ask Third Uncle. Maybe he would take her. Miss Cindy sang the song again, phrase by phrase, and the students echoed each phrase.

"You have done very well today. See you in the morning," she said, dismissing the class.

Mai walked down the beach, singing "Take me out to the ball game" softly to herself. Hiep was sitting in the tent eating a bowl of rice when she arrived back at camp.

"Hiep, what happened?" she asked.

"You were right," he said, suspending his chopsticks in midair. "She wouldn't listen."

"What did she say?" Mai asked, but Hiep just shook his head. "Did you see Minh? How are the children?"

"She's turned them against us. They ran and hid behind her when they saw me." Hiep ran his hands through his hair.

"Oh no," Mai moaned. How unfair of her. Somehow she would have to find Minh and speak to him when he was alone. Surely Minh didn't hate them. "What did she say?" Mai repeated.

"She chased me away with her broom before I could say anything. She's crazy." Hiep's voice rose.

"I knew you shouldn't go. I'm afraid of her." Mai sighed in despair, for she had grown to love the children, and it had been hard for her to leave them. Now Small Auntie would keep her from seeing them and Sang's ghost would haunt her. She didn't think life could get any worse. What were they going to do?

"Uncle Hiep, we must write Third Uncle right away. We

need to get out of here as soon as we can. Where's the money he sent? Let's go to the market and get a pen and paper."

"Shh, Mai." Hiep peered around the rice bag partition to see if anyone had come in, but there were only a few of the women outside, tending the cooking fires. "It's in here." He reached into the elastic waistband of his shorts and pulled out the American bill. "I wouldn't leave it in the tent. Someone might take it."

Mai smiled knowingly as she touched the waistband of her pants, where her lucky gold bracelet was hidden. He was right. She trusted Kien and Lan, but there were others just like Small Auntie who were interested only in money.

"I'll go to the market and we'll write Third Uncle a letter tonight. Maybe he can help."

Mai felt relieved at Hiep's words. Just then Kien came in, followed by Lan. Hiep stuffed the bill back in his pocket as Lan approached Mai.

"Mai, I was looking for you. Some of the girls are knitting and they said they would teach us how, if you'd like to learn."

Mai looked at Lan in confusion. Lan held a ball of yellow yarn in one hand and some knitting needles in the other. What did she need to knit for?

Lan explained. "You're going to America, where it snows. You'll need some warm clothes, some hats, some gloves, a scarf. That's what the girls are knitting. It's fun."

Mai shrugged her shoulders. "I'll try," she said, "but I've never been any good at needlework. My nanny tried to teach me embroidery, but I always poked my finger and made the stitches too big."

Lan laughed. "This is easier than embroidery and the needles aren't sharp. You'll need to get some yarn and needles at the market, though."

"Come with us, Lan," Hiep interrupted. "This afternoon. You can help Mai find what she needs."

Mai noticed the way Hiep's voice rose with excitement as he spoke to Lan. She looked over at Kien, who was talking to a round-faced young woman with high cheek bones, and a feeling of jealousy came over her as she turned to Lan, trying hard to ignore him.

"Oh, please come with us," she pleaded. Lan smiled and nodded her head in assent.

Ten

Later that afternoon, when the heat of the day had subsided and the leaves of the palm trees rustled from the beginnings of the onshore breeze, Mai, Lan, and Hiep headed for the market in the middle of the island near the Red Cross headquarters. Refugees squatted in the sand hawking pots and pans, cooking utensils, tin cups and plates, and cans of cooking oil, much of which had been sold to them by those fortunate enough to be leaving the island.

Mai was excited, for she had never been there, and she almost forgot about her nighttime apparition until they came near Small Auntie's boat, tilted to one side at the edge of the beach and the jungle. She stopped and wouldn't go any farther.

"What's wrong?" Lan asked as Mai stared at the boat.

"She had a nightmare about Small Auntie's husband. She thinks he's going to hurt us." Hiep motioned to Mai to keep walking, but she wouldn't, for it was not just the sight of the boat—the paint peeling from its sides, the wooden hull beginning to decompose in the tropical heat and humidity. Something was very peculiar. What was it? *The smell.* That was it. The smell of decay. Sang's ghost must be very close.

And then she saw him. Floating over the bow of the boat, staring at them.

"Look. There he is. By the boat," she screamed.

Sang's ghost moved toward them. Mai could see his face twisted in agony. "You can't escape me. I'm coming to get you," he called. And he started to run toward them.

"Hurry, Uncle Hiep. We've got to get away. He's after us." Mai turned around and bolted toward the jungle. Hiep and Lan ran after her. The ghost gave a haunting scream and disappeared.

"Mai, stop it. You are having delusions. Maybe I should take you to the clinic," called Hiep.

"Didn't you see him?" Mai crouched in fear, peering up at Hiep. "And couldn't you smell him?"

"I don't know what's wrong with her," Hiep said to Lan.

"Could it be malaria?" Lan suggested, touching Mai's forehead with her fingertips. Lan's touch was soothing to Mai, but she pushed Hiep's hand away.

"I don't have malaria and I'm not sick." She did not like to be treated like a child.

"The only thing I can smell is smoke and sea air," said Hiep. "Now come on. If you're not sick, then let's go to the market. This was your idea." He pulled Mai's arms and brought her to a standing position, then dragged her forward, past the boat. Mai noticed a woman's face, her eyes dark and angry, a murmuring sound coming from her lips, peering at them over the rails of the deck.

"Look, Uncle. It's Small Auntie. She sounds like she's casting a spell on us."

But Hiep continued walking despite Mai's protests, and before long the market came into view: the beach lined with men and women squatting in the sand, bamboo baskets before them filled with pots and pans, black with use, there for the asking if you only had money or something of value to trade. The sellers called to them when the trio stopped to inspect each basket.

Mai remembered going to Can Tho with her father, watching the fishermen hawk their wares at the floating market, the women with their *non-lás* covering their heads, their boats sinking low in the water from the weight of the coconuts, bananas, and dragon fruit. The sun had cast a pink spray on the early morning throng, on the stilt houses with thatched roofs that sat high on spindly legs along the river's edge. She remembered the taste of the warm egg noodle soup Father had bought her. Her favorite breakfast. Her stomach growled.

"You want a nice Timex watch? Very cheap," a young boy about Minh's age implored, holding up his arm, on which he displayed three watches.

Mai looked down at him and saw an empty T-shirt sleeve where his other arm should have been. Next to him was a young woman, maybe his mother, a basket in front of her piled high with dried fish, the tails crusted from the sun. Mai watched Hiep walk over to a blanket spread with pads of paper and pencils. He began to barter with a hunchbacked woman. He pulled the American bill with the *50* on it out of his waistband.

"Too big, too big. I can't take this," she complained,

shoving it back at him. Hiep looked around, wondering what to do.

She pointed to a fat, white-haired man sitting on a rickety wooden chair. He was blowing rings of smoke into the air from a cigarette he held between two gold teeth, his eyes hidden behind a pair of dark black sunglasses. "Take it over there. Get it changed," she said.

Hiep approached him. "Can you exchange this for me?" He held the worn American bill in the palm of his hand.

The man just grunted and pulled a wad of bills from his shirt, counted out a short pile, and handed them to Hiep. He took Hiep's money and slid it into his wad. Hiep started to ask him a question, but the man turned and blew a puff of smoke in the air, dismissing him.

Glancing at the bills in his hand, Hiep frowned and returned to the middle-aged woman.

She cackled at his bewilderment. "Of course he cheated you. Is that what you're wondering?"

Hiep picked up a pad of paper and a pencil and handed her a bill.

"One more," she demanded, sticking out her hand as Hiep frowned and pulled out another bill. She stuffed the money in the top of her blouse and gave him a gap-toothed smile. He clutched the pencil and paper and turned to Mai and Lan.

"You could have gotten it cheaper," Lan said, raising her eyebrows when they had stepped away from the woman.

Hiep didn't answer, just followed Lan to a gaunt young woman, with a child on her lap, selling balls of yarn and knitting needles, while Mai trailed behind, fascinated by the goods she saw in each basket.

The child, chewing on a strand of yarn, smiled at them. She looked like Nhu, with dainty fingers and toes, her hair a dark halo encircling her little round cheeks, her eyes dark and darting, two baby teeth protruding from her lower gums. Nhu. Would she ever get to see her again?

"Getting teeth," the woman explained, brushing a lock of hair out of the toddler's eyes. At that, the little girl, clad only in a ragged T-shirt, her golden bottom bare, started to screech and fling her feet.

"Could I hold her?" Mai asked.

"Here." With a sigh, the woman picked the child up under her arms and handed her to Mai, who knelt and took her. The tiny girl searched Mai's face with her large dark eyes and stopped crying while Mai held the small body against her chest and patted her back. The child's skin felt soft as silk against Mai's, and she could feel the tiny gasps subside as the child settled herself into her chest and lay her head on her shoulder.

"Shh. Shh," she whispered to her as she rocked back and forth. How she missed holding Nhu. She wondered if Nhu missed her. The girl's mother looked up at Mai and smiled with relief, and then turned her eyes to Lan, who was examining the knitting needles and the balls of yarn.

"What color would you like, Mai?" Lan asked. "This blue is pretty, or how about this green?"

Mai peered over the child's head and looked at the yarn. Red had always been her favorite color, but she couldn't see any red yarn, only blue and green. Perhaps the green. It reminded her of the banana trees and the mango grove behind her home on the Mekong. Blue reminded her of the ocean, which was all she ever saw when she looked out at the horizon searching for a glimpse of her homeland, and if she ever got off this island, she never wanted to see the ocean again. It surrounded the island, its deceptive aquamarine waters locking them in, confining them, stealing their freedom. A prison in paradise.

"Green," she said.

Lan took the ball of yarn and picked out some small knitting needles. "These will be good for making a warm hat or a scarf," she said.

"I'd like to make a scarf first," Mai said, imagining the cold wind of Chicago whipping around her neck.

Hiep bartered with the woman for a few minutes, and then handed her two bills. The woman smiled and pressed the knitting needles and yarn into Hiep's hands. Mai felt the child asleep on her shoulder and wished she didn't have to give her back. She stood in the sun, nuzzling the girl's head with her chin, comforted by the small body in her arms. How she wished she could rest like this in her mother's arms, safe and secure, unafraid, no one haunting her sleep.

"Goodbye, I have to go now," she whispered in the child's ear, handing her back to her mother. The toddler stirred and opened her lids briefly, her eyelashes dark and delicate, then closed them again, her bow-shaped lips forming a smile as her mother placed her on a blanket.

When Mai stood to leave, she saw a familiar small

figure talking to an old woman selling mangoes. His head was turned, but she could see his profile—the strong chin, the wide nose, and the shock of black hair that covered the back of his neck. His shoulders were narrow, his waist even thinner. A pair of navy shorts draped themselves around him, just below his knees where a pair of stick-like legs protruded. His tanned feet were bare. It was Minh. She hadn't seen him since his father died.

She crouched on the sand, pretending to examine the yarn so he would not see her. Lan and Hiep had already gone off in another direction. She wanted to talk to Minh. Would he run from her? She had to take that chance. She looked over at him. His back was to her. She walked over to him, wondering what she should say.

"Minh?" she said.

He turned, startled. His cheeks were sunken, his lips cracked and dry.

"Minh, how are you? I've been so worried about you." The words rushed out before she could stop them.

Minh just looked at her. Then he spoke. "I'm not supposed to talk to you." His eyes were hard, but his chin quivered.

This is so unfair, Mai thought. "Please, let me talk to you," she said.

Minh started to say something, but his eyes darted to the side and his head turned to look at Small Auntie. She was walking toward them, her face as dark as the storms that swept in over the ocean.

"I've got to go," he stammered, and left Mai standing in the sun staring at him.

Small Auntie yanked his arm and yelled at him. Mai wanted to tell Minh she was sorry, but Small Auntie shook her fist and barked some angry words at her she couldn't understand. Embarrassed, afraid, Mai looked around for Hiep and Lan. Some of the sellers were packing up their goods to leave. A few people hovered over baskets, bartering. Where were her friends? They hadn't left her, had they?

"Mai, where have you been?" Hiep's irritated voice echoed in her ear, his lean frame looming over her, his lips pursed, and she looked up at him with relief.

"I saw Minh. I tried to talk to him and then Small Auntie came along. She took him away."

Lan put her arm around Mai's shoulder and pulled her close, her hot breath fanning Mai's cheek. "You just have to let them grieve. Sometimes people need to be left alone."

Mai looked at her and pulled away. Lan didn't understand; no one did.

"Let's get in line for our food. It's time."

Mai brightened, knowing that Lan was trying to take her mind off of Minh. But it didn't work. She had to talk to Minh. As they left the market, she clutched the ball of yarn and knitting needles in her hands and plotted how she would be able to talk to him without Small Auntie finding out. Maybe Minh would be the one to intercede for them with Sang's ghost. She would go to see him when he was alone. Yes, that was what she would do.

She glanced at Hiep, who was walking with Lan, the pencil balanced behind his ear, the writing paper stuffed in the back pocket of his pants. Tonight they would write a letter to

Third Uncle. He might be able to get their names moved to the top of the immigration list. She passed by the tall timber pole with the metal loudspeaker atop it that every morning blared out the latest list of those chosen to leave, and a remnant of hope returned.

Eleven

Mai lay in her hammock, her short legs draped over the side, her thin arms resting on her chest, watching Hiep hunched over the pad of paper, his fingers tight around the pencil, writing to Third Uncle. The oil candle flickered. Light was a precious commodity on the island, for when the moon waned, the tent was as dark as the hold of the ship they had crossed on.

Hiep had saved some tin cans from their rations and, with a piece of string and some cooking oil from the market, he had made a candle by pouring the oil in the can and draping the strand of string in the oil for a wick. Using a stick from the cooking fire, he lit the candle as Mai watched. Back home, their family had been the first in the village to have electricity, but now Mai had become used to living without it; she hadn't missed it until Sang's ghost had come to haunt her, and now she moved closer to the light, suddenly wary of the dark and what might be lurking there.

The wind had started to moan outside, and Mai knew that the monsoons, the seasonal southwest winds, would soon be lashing the island. At home the monsoons had brought the rain that filled the rice paddies so that the villagers could plant the slender green plants for the new crop. When the storms came, she had been safe inside her brick home listening to the drops drumming the tile roof. Here there were no rice paddies and only a thin tarp overhead to shelter them from the constant downpour. But they could put out their tin cans to catch the rain. No more shortage of drinking water.

"Tell Third Uncle about Sang's ghost," she pleaded. "Tell him we need to get out of here." Hiep's face was tense, and, ignoring her, he continued to write.

They had to get away from Small Auntie too. When she had first grabbed them from the crowd stumbling onshore from the fishing trawler, Mai had felt relief and gratitude, but when Small Auntie had asked for payment, and refused to let them stay with her unless they paid her more, Mai could see that her smile had only masked the greediness in her grasping heart.

She watched Hiep form precise Chinese characters with his pencil for as long as she could, but, exhausted by the lack of rest the night before, she succumbed to a fitful sleep.

That night, Sang's ghost appeared along with all the children—Minh, Diep, Huong, Nhu—and Small Auntie, swirling around in a dark mist, calling to her in a clamoring chorus. She was standing on the ocean's shore, the white-tipped waves crashing at her feet as if they were attacking her, the palm trees furiously waving their fronds, the biting sand swirling in circles in the air. She tried to decipher what each person was saying, and then realized that their mouths were all forming the same words: "You will be punished."

She cowered on the beach, whimpering, "No, no, it's not our fault. You must understand." But their hollow red eyes pierced her with their anger and she covered her face with her hands, listening to the whoosh of their bodies circling over her head, echoing "Mai, Mai."

Just then Kien, flashing a silver sword, strode into her dream, yelling, "Leave her alone, evil spirits." They fled from him, dissolving into the sea, as he sheathed his sword and folded his sturdy arms around Mai, pulling her close.

A warm glow enveloped her when his gentle hands caressed her. She reached up to touch his face but he disappeared, her frantic hands raking through the air.

"Kien, don't leave me," she called, but he didn't answer.

Neither did the others, and after a restless sleep where a large eagle with Small Auntie's face landed on her head and pulled her eyes out with its talons, she woke in the morning, her body limp. Would no one protect them? She stepped onto the dirt floor of their tent and slipped her feet into her dép before walking outside.

"Did you finish the letter?" she asked Hiep, pouring a cup of water into a pot fashioned from an oil can. She added a handful of dry rice to it and balanced it on a rock over the cooking fire. Hiep pulled a bent envelope from his shorts pocket and showed it to her.

"It's right here. I'm going to take it down to the Red Cross this morning."

"Do you think it will do any good?" she asked, stirring the rice with a stick so it wouldn't burn.

"Maybe. Third Uncle is a very important man."

Mai thought about what Hiep said. Yes, Third Uncle was a very important man, but she wondered how important he could be in a new country where he didn't know anyone. In his letter, he hadn't told them what he was doing. Maybe he was too ashamed. She could picture him overseeing the rice farmers for her father, but in America, in the city, he might be reduced to sweeping the streets, or washing vegetables in the dank cellar of a Chinese restaurant. She hoped he could help them, but what if he couldn't? Then what would they do?

Mai looked up at Hiep, who was standing by the fire with the letter in his hands staring at her. There was something he wasn't telling her. "What is it, Uncle Hiep? What's wrong?"

Hiep cleared his throat, shifting his eyes to see if anyone was listening. A few young women squatted by cooking fires several feet away from them. "I saw Sang's ghost last night," he whispered in her ear, cupping his hand to his mouth to keep his words from floating away.

Mai gaped at Hiep, her throat dry, unable to speak. So she had not imagined Sang's ghost. He was real.

The smell of burnt rice brought Mai out of her stupor and she trembled as she lifted the pot from the fire. "What did he look like?" she asked.

"He had on the ragged shorts he died in, he was fuming, and he called my name. I'm sure it was him."

"Hiep, mail that letter right away. Talk to the man at the Red Cross tent. Maybe there's a way we can get off this island and go somewhere else, a place where Sang and Small Auntie can't find us. What about Pulau Bidong? Isn't that where Fourth Uncle landed?"

Pulau Bidong was a much larger refugee camp. When it became overcrowded, the escape boats were turned away and sent to the much smaller island, Pulau Tengah, instead. Fourth Uncle and his family had escaped before Mai and Hiep, and they'd been overjoyed to find his name on the list of refugees tacked to the Red Cross bulletin board. But one of the Red Cross workers had told them that Pulau Bidong had over twenty thousand refugees on it and would not be taking any more.

Hiep sighed. "They made it, but that camp is full. I'll go send this letter. Then I'll pick up some food. We've got to stock up. The monsoons will be here soon, and it will be impossible to get to the middle of the island."

"Here, drink some water before you go." Mai offered Hiep a tin can filled with water, but he shook his head. She twisted a strand of stray hair around her finger as Hiep turned to go. What would become of them? She didn't know if she could bear to wait several years to leave this island, as some of the others had.

She thought of the ones who had given up hope. Suicide. A young man whose pregnant wife and three children had drowned on the journey across the ocean had only lasted a month on the island. Alone and depressed, he had walked into the sea at night, two weeks ago. The tide had returned his bloated body to the beach three days later, where it had lain in a tide pool, its filmy salt-crusted eyes wide open, staring into the morning sun, waiting to be discovered by the first passer-by.

She had not seen his body, but she had heard Lan and

the others talking about it one evening when they were sitting around after dinner. "I would never be that depressed." Lan's voice had wavered, her words unconvincing.

Mai had heard of suicide from her father. A elderly village official had been accused of stealing tax money, and rather than face Mai's father, he had taken poison in his tea. Mai's father had sternly denounced the man and the act of suicide.

"You should not take your fate into your own hands. Chu Phu has brought shame on himself and his family. No one will want to marry into that family now. He has brought a stain on their name."

Mai remembered these words, but she found it hard to be hopeful, and she understood how easy it would be to give up. Maybe, in some cases, suicide was not as wrong as Father had said, but she could never do anything that would dishonor her family.

Twelve

A few days later, after breakfast, Mai heard Lan and some of the other girls seated in the sand, giggling, as they held their balls of yarn in their laps and looped strands around the points of their needles.

Lan gestured for her to come over. "Mai, get your knitting needles and yarn. Come on."

Mai groaned. She did not feel like gossiping with the girls. Not today. She had too many worries. She ducked behind the rice bag partition that separated their hammocks from the others and crawled into hers.

A soft voice called to her. "Mai, are you in there? What's the matter?" Lan peeked around the partition, and Mai looked up at her. "Still worried about that ghost?"

Mai could not tell whether Lan was teasing her or not, but she didn't answer.

"You know, Mai, the best way to get rid of a ghost is to be around people. They like to haunt you when you're alone." Lan stroked her hand. "Come on out and learn to knit. You can't lie in here all day."

Lan sounded like her nanny, Ba Du, who had always

tried to comfort her and cheer her up when she was sad. Ba Du had been Mai's constant companion since she was born. She had nursed her, rocked her, dressed her, read her stories, and loved her when her mother had been too busy waiting on Grandmother to pay any attention to her. Ba Du. She had called her Du for short.

Mai laughed when she remembered how stubborn she had been. She had hated baths when she was little and had screamed when Du tried to put her in the washtub. The water had chilled her bare limbs at first, even though Du would mix a kettle of hot water from the brick kitchen stove with the cold river water from the clay tank. How patient Du had been with her. Where was she now, Mai wondered? Was she still alive? How she missed her.

Enough daydreaming. She had to get ready to go to America. She could not lie here and feel sorry for herself. Father would be disappointed in her if she let Small Auntie and Sang's ghost frighten her. Somehow she would have to appease Sang's wandering spirit.

Mai found the basket she had put her balled yarn and knitting needles in and walked with Lan to the knitting circle in the sand. The girls looked up as she approached them.

"Sit down," Kim said, as she patted the ground next to her. "We'll teach you how to knit."

Kim, a short plump girl with pockmarked cheeks, sat next to Ngoc, Lan's older sister. Ngoc, a tall girl with bony arms and legs, a flat chest, and a long neck, didn't have a spare ounce of flesh on her. She rarely smiled, unlike Lan, who could be heard laughing even when she was hauling the heaviest water buckets from the well.

"Is it hard?" Mai asked, lowering herself to the spot near Kim.

Kim shook her head. "You just have to learn two stitches and be able to count."

Mai liked Kim. Although she was a university student like the others, she treated Mai as an equal, unlike some of the girls who thought she was just a child. She and Kim had talked one night after dinner and Kim had told her about her family, her mother's death from malaria, and her father's imprisonment in a re-education camp. Like Mai, she was Chinese, her father a wealthy landowner whose land had been conscripted by the Communists.

Kim's brother, Tuan, often joined them in the evening after dinner when they sat talking around the fire. Mai thought he was handsome with his wire frame glasses, angular cheekbones, and squared jaw. Although he had little to say, when he did say something, Mai noticed that everyone listened to him. He knew a lot about the history of Vietnam, the war, and why the Communists had won.

"The Viet Cong have always had the hearts of the peasants. They are the only ones who have wanted to reunite the country. Ho Chi Minh, their great leader, instilled so much nationalism in them and they fought hard. South Vietnam never had a chance once the Americans pulled out," Tuan said. Mai knew little about politics, but Tuan spoke with authority.

As she looked at her knitting needles, Mai's cheeks turned red. Why was she always afraid to try new things? She had tried to learn to cook when they came to the island, but all she ever managed to do was warm the beef stew or peas from the cans or boil a little rice over the cooking fire. When they had fresh food on Thursday, like chicken or bok choy, Lan cooked for them. She would show the girls now that she could do something well.

Kim ignored her embarrassment and proceeded to show her how to hold the needles and loop the yarn around them. Mai tried to concentrate, but she kept thinking about Sang's ghost and his threat of revenge.

"There are two stitches, knit and purl. Hold the needle like this and loop the yarn this way. Then bring the needle through like this."

Mai tried to do what she was being shown, but the needle slipped out of the yarn loop. She looked over at Lan and Ngoc, who were busy weaving their needles in and out of the yarn. She looped the yarn around the needle again and pulled the loop through, and then it came to her—the tigers.

Of course. That's how they would keep Sang's ghost away. She jumped up from the circle, clutching her needles and yarn, and ran to the tent. Where was that paper that Hiep had bought? What had he done with the pencil? She could hear Lan calling. "Mai, what's the matter?"

"I just remembered something. I can't knit now. Maybe later," she answered.

Mai rummaged in Hiep's hammock, and there, underneath his extra T-shirt, were the pencil and pad of paper. The paper was plain white, about the size of the composition book she'd used at school, but it would do. She carried the paper and pencil outside and found a flat black rock to sit on.

She stared out at the panorama of the yellow sky dipping into the jade green sea and closed her eyes, trying to remember what they had looked like. Then she opened her eyes and began to draw: first the head, and then the long sleek body coming out of the drawing as if it were ready to pounce.

She sketched slowly, adding the sharp teeth, the small ears, and the long tail. She made thin black marks for the stripes, and when she had finished, she held the drawing up in front of her. It almost looked like a tiger. She added a few more stripes, and, satisfied with the first drawing, began a second. One tiger would not do. She would need two.

When she finished the second tiger, she carried the drawings to her hammock and, unraveling a piece of string from the rice bag partition, hung one tiger picture above her hammock and one above Hiep's hammock.

At home, outside their bedrooms, Father had hung pictures of tigers to keep the evil spirits away from them. He told them the tiger was the strongest and most vicious animal in the Chinese zodiac and that it would protect them. He had also told her that he was glad she had not been born in the year of the tiger, for girls born under its sign were too domineering and hard to marry off.

Mai felt the tension in her melt as she looked at the tigers. Their mouths were open wide, displaying their sharp teeth, and their bodies were curved and poised to pounce. She knew they could keep Sang's ghost away. Mai couldn't wait to see Hiep; he would be so thankful to her.

But when Hiep came in, his hands in his pockets and a scowl on his face, he barely noticed the tigers.

"Hiep, look. Remember the tigers outside my bedroom? That's the answer. I drew some tigers for us. Now Sang can't harm us."

Hiep lay down in his hammock and looked at the tiger face staring at him. "I had forgotten, Mai. You're right." He groaned and reached for his side.

"What's the matter, Hiep? Did you hurt yourself today?"

"I don't think so, but my right side has been aching all day. I think I'll rest awhile." He closed his eyes and grimaced as he sought to get comfortable in his hammock.

"Let me warm up some dinner for you." Mai picked up a can of beef stew.

"I'm not really hungry. Just leave me alone."

Hiep turned his face away from her and put his arms over his head. Mai glanced at the tigers, admiring her work and hurt that Hiep had been so abrupt with her. She didn't always feel good either, but she would never treat him with disrespect. Of course, he was her elder, but she cooked for him and washed his clothes and took care of him. He should be grateful for her help. She left the tent and saw Kien coming down the beach, his eyes squinting in the sun, his arms swinging at his side. Kien. She looked at him and a smile touched her lips.

"Mai, I've been looking for you. Want to go look for firewood with me?"

Mai brightened. She needed to get away from Hiep and the tent. "Sure, I need some for this evening's fire."

Kien walked alongside her as they crossed the sand and passed by the coconut palms and low-lying grasses at the edge of the jungle. She would never go very far into the jungle. Beyond were the mountains, rising straight up into the tropical sky. Who knew what kind of wild animals might be there? She had heard that boars ran wild on some of the islands.

There might even be some tigers. Pictures of them were fine, but she would not like to run into a real one. A seven-year-old boy in her village had been eaten by a tiger early one morning as he looked for his ball on the edge of the jungle. All that was left of him was a sandal with a bloody foot in it, the stumps of two toes, surrounded by tiger tracks. Father had warned them never to go into the jungle by themselves. She had had nightmares for weeks about being eaten by a tiger.

She glanced up at Kien as they padded through the tall thickets of bamboo, stopping at intervals to pick up broken branches to pile in their arms. Kien held his head up when he walked, not afraid of anything. The only sound Mai heard was the pounding of her heart as she thought of Sang's ghost and what he might do to them.

"What's the matter, Mai? Is something bothering you? You're so quiet." Kien looked up at her as he stooped to pick up a small twig. *No one else notices me the way he does*, Mai thought. She wiped her face with the back of her hand.

"It's Sang's ghost. He visited Hiep too. He's real and he wants to punish us. We wrote my uncle to see if he could get us out of here soon, and then I drew paper tigers to scare Sang's ghost away. But I don't know if any of this is going to work, and if it doesn't, he may kill us."

Her words came out in a torrent. *Oh, no.* She looked at him. Would he believe her? Kien's eyes narrowed and he closed his rough fingers around her hand. She drew it away, embarrassed.

"Don't be afraid. I'll protect you from his ghost." Kien thrust out his thin chest and tried to look brave like a tiger.

Mai doubted that even Kien could protect them, but she remembered her dream where he had come and encircled her with his arm, and she felt comforted.

"You do believe me, don't you, Kien? Ghosts are real. It's not some silly superstition. Grandfather told me about their wandering spirits."

"I do," said Kien. "But I haven't seen Sang's ghost."

"He's here. On this island. I've seen him three times."

She stayed close to him as they continued picking up wood. When their arms were full, they carried the branches back to the tent and dropped them near the three rocks surrounding the fire pit.

Hiep was not in his hammock when Mai pushed the rice bag partition aside to check on him. What was wrong with him? He had probably just pulled a muscle when he was working at the well. He needed a little time to heal and he would be fine.

She remembered the time she'd run in a race at school. The ground had been uneven and she had stumbled, fallen, and hurt her side, losing the race. For several days, she'd flinched every time she took a step, the pain surging down her side. But then she slowly felt better. Yes, time would heal him.

For the next several days, Hiep was not himself, rarely talking, coming back to the tent late and eating a few grains of rice, then going to sleep in his hammock without a word to anyone. His once-bright eyes turned dim and his walk was slow and sad. Mai had tried to talk to him, but he brushed her away.

"Something's wrong with Hiep," Lan said. "He won't eat. And he won't talk to me. I'm worried about him."

"I am too," Mai said. Lan followed her to Hiep's hammock.

"What's the matter, Hiep? Aren't you feeling well? You can't go on like this. Please talk to me." Mai's voice cracked as she reached forward to touch Hiep's forehead.

Lan offered him a cup of water. He turned his head away. Mai saw that his eyes and skin had a yellow hue, like the bananas in her father's orchard.

"I'm just a little tired. I need to sleep," he groaned.

The next morning Mai heard him retching, and she peered down to see him with vomit spewing from his mouth like a fountain to the floor of the tent, his body turned to the side to avoid soiling his hammock.

"Hiep, let me help you outside," she offered, but his answer was another retch of his body, with one more stream of vomit dribbling down his bare chest. She grabbed his arms, but he was like one of the large boulders on the beach and she couldn't move him. His eyelids fluttered and his eyes rolled back, but he didn't respond. What should she do?

The acrid smell of vomit overcame her and she stepped outside the partition to look for help. She tried not to panic. Was Hiep dying, or had he just eaten some spoiled food? Spoiled food wouldn't make his eyes and skin yellow, would it?

Mai looked around. The island was just starting to stir.

Usually, she loved the way the billowing clouds filled the once-empty sky, signaling the beginning of the rainy season after the long dry spell. She could hear the soft melodious voices of the young women as they built their cooking fires and began the morning ritual of boiling rice for breakfast. She could smell the salt air as it rode the waves to the beach and feel the sizzle of the morning sun as it started to fry the day. Lan was adding twigs one at a time to her cooking fire.

"Lan, Lan," Mai called, afraid to leave Hiep. Lan looked up and Mai called again. "Help. Something's the matter with Hiep."

Lan pulled the pot from the fire and ran to Mai, who led her to where Hiep lay motionless, covered in vomit, sprawled on his back in his hammock. Kim appeared at the edge of the partition.

"I heard you call," she said as Lan bent over Hiep and softly whispered, "Hiep."

No response. Mai felt his forehead. She opened one of his eyes. A yellow circle surrounded its pupil, matching the shade of his skin. The stench of Hiep's vomit made her feel lightheaded. Sick people frightened her and all she wanted to do was get away, but she summoned up her courage.

"We need to get him to the doctor. He's very sick." She choked back a sob. Kim had gotten a can of water and a cloth, which Lan took from her.

In a steady voice, Lan said, "Get someone strong. Tuan. Hiep can't walk all that way."

Mai watched Lan dip the cloth in the cold water, and wipe the vomit from Hiep's face and chest, her hand stroking his skin tenderly, her face turning crimson. Hiep opened his eyes for a brief moment, looked up at her, and then, sighing, closed them. Kim disappeared from the tent to search for Tuan, but Mai stayed, afraid to leave Hiep.

Kim returned several minutes later with Tuan at her side, her eyebrows knit with concern.

Mai glanced at Tuan. "Please help us."

Lan dipped the cloth in the water again and brushed a fly from Hiep's forehead. He did not stir.

"Please don't let him die," Mai moaned as she sank to the ground, her legs folding under her.

"Don't worry, Mai. We'll get him to the doctor. He'll make him well," said Tuan, touching her on the shoulder and then leaning over to pick up Hiep, whose yellowed eyes were staring up at him. "Can you hold on to me?" Tuan asked.

Hiep gave a silent nod as Lan placed his limp arms around Tuan's neck. Tuan bent over and grabbed Hiep above the knees so that he could carry him on his back. Tuan's neck muscles popped out like the roots of a mangrove tree as he stumbled from under the brown tarp, shifting Hiep's dead weight so that it was distributed evenly.

Mai, revived, trailed behind him, holding on to Hiep's dangling foot in an attempt to lighten Tuan's load. Why hadn't she realized that Hiep was very sick? Tuan stumbled, then regained his balance as Hiep's half-conscious body lurched to one side.

Mai murmured prayers to Great-grandfather and any other ancestor she thought might be listening. She had never been sure if the gods listened or even existed. Sang's spirit was at work on the island, and it was very powerful. She had thought the tigers would keep it away, but they hadn't. Maybe she hadn't drawn them right. Maybe they hadn't been fierce enough. If only Father were here; he would know what to do.

She remembered the bridge across the river to the island where their tea house had been. Father had had the servants place the large stone blocks of the bridge in a zigzag pattern so that the evil spirits could not follow them across. When she crossed, she would peer over her shoulder as she held Father's hand to see if they were following them. Father would look down and squeeze her hand, saying, "Don't worry. They're not following us," as if he knew why she was looking.

Would Sang's ghost be able to follow Hiep if Hiep left the island?

Just then Tuan stumbled and fell to the ground, pitching Hiep forward. Hiep landed with a thump and a groan. Tuan remained on the ground, panting, streaks of perspiration running down his forehead. Mai yelped and ran over to Hiep, who was lying motionless.

"Is he all right?" Tuan asked. "I didn't see that rock."

Hiep was lying face down in the sand, his arms sprawled to the side, his legs bent underneath him. Mai moved his head to one side and saw that his eyes were open and he was breathing. She fell back as the sour smell of sweat and vomit hit her.

The sand felt like hot needles as the sun's rays broiled the island. Ahead of them, Mai could see the ocean cutting its way into the island and the black rock path they took to cross it. She squinted up at the sky; the billowing clouds had begun to change into dark ominous shapes. The monsoons were coming; they had to cross the water before the torrential rains began or the way would be impassable. Mai scanned the forty-foot divide. The water was higher than usual.

"The clouds." She pointed to the sky.

Tuan looked up and ran to Hiep. He leaned over, lifted him over his shoulder, and stood upright, trudging down the beach while Mai loped after him, amazed at his sudden burst of energy. The water loomed before them, and the dark rocks beckoned them.

Tuan stepped out onto the first one, jagged and oblong, jutting up near the shore, its top flat and smooth, and Mai squeezed her eyes closed. When she didn't hear a splash, she opened them and spied Tuan, moving slowly like a water buffalo, extend his left leg up to a smaller round rock that was partially submerged by the waves. As if he were walking through a mine field, he moved from one rock to another, twelve in all, stopping at each one to shift the human burden on his back and regain his balance.

A white-tipped wave pounded them as Tuan stepped to the last rock. Tuan's torso tilted, his bare knees buckled, and his feet started to slide into the water. He tried to grab Hiep, but the force of the wave was too great and Hiep slipped from his back and plunged into the ocean.

Mai screamed, "Don't let him drown," but the waves crashed and her words fell into the water.

She could see Hiep's frightened eyes and the shock of his dark hair rising above the surface as Tuan lay prone, his stomach pressed hard into the rock, reaching out to him.

Hiep disappeared, and then his round head bobbed to the surface and she could see Tuan, in the water, his arm around Hiep, dragging him up the rocky bank. Tuan tumbled Hiep gently onto the sand and beckoned to Mai, who stood rooted as a palm tree on the far bank.

"I can't do it," she called.

Tuan turned back to Hiep and pulled him to a sitting position. He waved again to Mai, motioning her to come. Mai knew that she had to cross the water. Hiep needed her. She could see Tuan kneeling in the sand, trying to hoist Hiep on his back.

"Wait for me, I'm coming." She stepped onto the first rock. If Tuan could cross carrying Hiep, surely she could make it by herself. She felt her lucky gold bracelet in her waistband and cautiously moved to the next rock as the warm water lapped around her feet. A seagull flapped its wings above her and then dove down to the ocean. She heard the splash and smiled to herself. An omen. She spread her arms like a bird's wings and soared to the next rock, a smooth boulder big enough to sit on. She would be like the seagull and fly across the water, unafraid. She could see the leafy bushes on the distant bank. The waves had subsided and the gull was swimming along in the water beside her, dipping its black beak in the sea and then lifting its white head to look at her. She leaped to the next rock, its surface slick from seaweed, and steadied herself, her body pitching forward. The gull paddled ahead of her, beckoning her on.

She remembered her father's words: *You must survive.* By now her fear had disappeared, and she crossed to the next rock, light of feet. Realizing she was almost across, she called to Tuan and the seagull, "I'm coming." She felt the strong grip of Tuan's hands dragging her up the bank and depositing her next to Hiep, and, turning her head, noticed the seagull circling above her like a kite against the azure sky. *Thank you*, she mouthed, and she watched the bird sail away toward the sun-dappled waves.

Thirteen

Together, Mai and Tuan trudged down the beach, Hiep, like a large bag of rice, on Tuan's bent back, moaning softly with each step. Their goal was the large Red Cross tent, the finish line where throngs of refugees sat on the ground outside waiting for their names to be called for immigration.

A bent old man with a straggly moustache eyed them as they approached. A baby squalled as he dug for his mother's breast. A teen-aged girl held a squirmy toddler on her lap. Every day, a few lucky people left. Someday soon she hoped their names would be called.

She followed Tuan as he entered the clinic and laid Hiep on the ground, then approached a tiny woman with crooked teeth and dressed in a soiled white uniform who was sitting on a wooden bench behind a small table. Tuan's chest was heaving, his breath coming in short gasps. Mai sat by Hiep and propped his head on her lap, her eyes focused on the woman and Tuan. She felt the weight of Hiep's head on her leg and raised her hand to brush his hair off his forehead. She could see his eyelids closed, feel his breathing soft and regular against her, and the heat of his body. A pain cut through her, running down her chest. She sat very still, her back aching, her head throbbing, her mind a muddle of fear and confusion.

"Is the doctor in?" Tuan asked.

The woman, her head bent over a notebook, did not look up. Tuan waited, his hands clasped in front of him, trying to be patient and polite, but Mai could see the muscles on the back of his neck tighten and turn red. *What is wrong with that woman?* The pain in Mai's chest grew sharper. The woman didn't answer but kept on reading. Tuan cleared his throat and coughed. Mai swatted the flies that crawled across Hiep's face and prayed that he would not die. The woman frowned at them, closed her book, and disappeared behind a partition. Tuan turned toward Mai and Hiep and balled his fists. Mai could feel the anger rising in her. They had come all this way to be ignored. If Hiep didn't get help soon, he might die. That woman was Vietnamese but she was just like the soldiers; she didn't care. It was just a job to her.

"Any more patients today?"

The tallest man Mai had ever seen appeared from behind the partition, wearing a white coat over his drab, knee-length shorts. A gray stethoscope dangled like a snake from his neck, and he carried a small black bag in his left hand. He must be American, but Mai was surprised at his flawless Vietnamese. Mai had seen a stethoscope before, when their family doctor had come to their house to tend to grandfather.

Mai spoke up. "It's my uncle. He's very sick. Can you help him?"

The doctor, a fringe of blond hair ringing his sunburned

scalp, his eyes as blue as the brightest sky, his damp white cheeks looking as if someone had painted large red circles on them, knelt down next to Hiep and took his pulse. Then he pried Hiep's eyelids open with his fingers.

"How long has he been like this?" he asked.

Mai looked at Tuan, afraid to answer. Finally, she said, "Several days. But we didn't know he was so sick."

The doctor nodded and barked some orders through the opening in the partition. The tiny woman they had first encountered came out. "Make up a cot for this man."

The woman nodded and scurried off to obey his orders.

"Can you help me carry him to the back? He's seriously dehydrated."

Tuan nodded and grabbed Hiep's shoulders. The doctor lifted Hiep's feet and together they carried Hiep to a small canvas cot in a partitioned area where the woman was busy preparing a syringe. The doctor covered Hiep with a lightweight blanket, swabbed Hiep's arm with alcohol, and injected some medicine into his veins. Mai watched as he wiped the area with alcohol again.

"This may help him. He's very sick. Tell me what happened."

Mai proceeded to relate the events of the last few days—her uncle's fatigue, the pain in his right side, and the nausea and vomiting. Tuan watched, taking in every word.

"We'll have to keep him here overnight. If he hasn't improved by morning we'll have to send him over to the hospital on the mainland. He hasn't had any convulsions, has he?" Mai gave him a puzzled look.

The doctor explained. "If his brain starts to swell, it can cause him to lose control of his body and shake all over. That is not a good sign."

"No, I don't think so," Mai answered, still not sure what a convulsion was. She wanted to ask the doctor what had happened to Hiep, why was he sick. Was it something he had caught? But she waited, self-conscious, frightened, chewing the fingernail on her left thumb. She had never spoken to a doctor before.

She was afraid to say anything about Sang's ghost. She knew the doctor wouldn't believe that a ghost could have caused Hiep's illness. But that was because he was American. If you were Vietnamese, you would know that the wandering ghosts caused lots of bad luck.

"He appears to have hepatitis. Jaundice. Yellow skin and eyes caused by the liver starting to fail."

Mai summoned her courage and interrupted in a whisper. "How did he get it?"

"It's a water-borne disease. The drinking water here isn't very clean. We've had a lot of these cases. We'll keep a close eye on him."

The confidence in the doctor's voice did not dull the pain in Mai's chest and she began to cry, covering her face, embarrassed at her outburst.

Wiping her tears away with the backs of her hands, she asked, "Can I stay with him?"

Before the doctor could answer, Tuan interrupted. "I'll stay with him. You go on back to camp and rest."

The doctor nodded in agreement. "I think it would be better if your friend stayed with him."

Mai hated to leave Hiep. Maybe she could just sleep outside the tent so she could check on him once in a while. Sang's ghost could have followed them to the clinic.

As if he could hear her thoughts, the doctor said, "You can stay for a while, but he really needs to sleep."

Mai knew the doctor would be going back to the mainland after lunch and he wouldn't know how long she stayed. She and Tuan walked over to see Hiep now resting peacefully on the cot, his arms folded across his chest.

"You'd better line up for food and then get back to camp and let them know we made it," Tuan said, scratching his chin.

"I'm not going anywhere. I need to stay and look after Hiep." The words came out of her mouth, not her heart, for she could still feel that dull pain running down the middle of her chest. She pressed her hand against her chest, trying to stop the pain.

"I'll stay. It's better if you go." Tuan put his hand on her shoulder. He walked outside with her.

"No, you need to take the food back to camp. I'll get mine and eat right here. I'll come back later. I'm so grateful to you. I could never have carried Uncle Hiep here." Mai could feel the tears ready to come again and she willed them back. She didn't want to show him how weak she was.

"I'll come and check on you this evening," Tuan said. Bowing, he reluctantly walked away from her and over to the food line. She sighed. He was so handsome with his high cheekbones and finely chiseled chin, and he was as kind as he was handsome.

She sat down on the hard sand, pressing her back on the hot canvas tent. She was sure that Sang's ghost had finally succeeded in punishing Hiep and he was not going to get better.

The tigers.

"Tuan, Tuan," she called.

Tuan turned around with a puzzled look on his face and retraced his steps. "What's the matter, Mai?"

"I have a favor to ask. Could you go in our tent and bring the tiger pictures by our hammocks? I need them right away."

"Of course, Mai." Tuan hurried back to the food line before he missed his turn.

Mai could tell that Tuan didn't understand her request, but she didn't want to explain. She would hang the tigers on the tent wall next to Hiep's cot. Maybe that would work.

She looked around at the clusters of men, women, and children lined up for the noon food. The men stood without talking, their empty hands dangling by their sides, their eyes averted as if they were embarrassed to be waiting for a handout. The women's voices had a singsong sound as they called to their children, who played in the sandy earth at their feet or darted in and out of the line, unaware of the desperation of their circumstances.

Mai's stomach rumbled but she ignored it. She'd just lie here and rest, she thought to herself, curling up in a shady spot outside where the tent cast its shadow on the ground, all her energy evaporated. The sand was cooler here, and she could feel a breeze starting to come in from the ocean. The leaves rustled in the nearby jungle. The voices around her melded into a single drone as her head touched the sand

and she stretched out her aching limbs. Inside the clinic, she could hear the doctor giving directions to the nurse, something about keeping an eye on Hiep. A fly landed on her nose and tickled it. She was too tired to brush it away. A pair of men's feet walked by her, attached to hairy legs, followed by two pairs of children's bare feet, caked with dirt, their tiny toenails black as the earth.

At first she thought someone had spilled a bucket of water on her. She moved to get out of the way, but the water poured down harder and faster as the wind swirled around her. When she opened her eyes, the sky seemed to descend to the earth, angry and dark, spilling sheets of warm torrential rains.

Mai turned her parched mouth to catch the drops pounding on her, too tired and depressed to move. The monsoons had arrived.

Fourteen

As she lay there, a cold hand reached down and inched its way along the waistband of Mai's pants, stopping at the bulge where she hid her gold bracelet. Long, slender fingers with jagged nails tugged at the jewelry and scratched her stomach.

Mai jerked to a sitting position and beheld Small Auntie, a startled, gap-toothed expression on her face, fumbling with her bracelet in the pouring rain. She could smell Small Auntie's foul breath as she grabbed her wrist and yelled, "Stop, thief!"

But no one heard, and Small Auntie, her face changing to a smirk, wrenched her arm away from Mai and ran, the bracelet clutched in her hands, her short body weaving across the sand and through the downpour into the dense bushes.

Mai, her soaked pants and blouse plastered to her body, struggled to her feet and raced after her, but stumbled on a fallen palm branch and sprawled in a pool of warm rain water. Where had Small Auntie come from? Why was she out in the rain, and how had she known about the bracelet in Mai's waistband? Mai wanted to pursue her, but she'd disappeared in the storm. She pulled up her blouse and saw a long bloody scratch.

A pair of black military boots approached her and stopped two feet away. Mai peeked up at a glowering Malaysian soldier covered by a rain poncho, a sticklike shape beneath it. Mai knew it was his rifle. She was afraid of the soldiers; she remembered how one had beaten the man who had stolen rice from the young woman at the food distribution center. She lowered her eyes, hoping the soldier would not notice her, but he had and growled and kicked some sand at her, then walked away laughing as if she were a stray dog.

Mai brushed the sand from her pants and clenched her teeth. She wished Small Auntie had died in the well with her husband. If only she'd never met her. She had brought nothing but bad luck.

The late afternoon sun finally broke through the storm clouds, a steamy heat rising from the ground as the rain subsided. The coconut palms were freshly washed, drops of water falling from their leafy fronds. Mai peered through the entrance of the clinic. No one was at the table. She wanted to see Hiep. She would think about her bracelet later. She crept into the tent and lifted the canvas flap behind the desk where his cot was. A strong medicinal smell mixed with the stifling heat made her gag, and she realized she had eaten nothing since morning. She ran outside and vomited on the ground near the entrance.

She wiped her face with her blouse and, cupping her hands over her mouth and her nose, edged back in, determined to visit Hiep. She could see his back through the faded green mosquito netting covering him. Lifting the netting, she saw his smooth lids closed, his gaunt face drawn, his thin chapped lips partially open, and she heard the soft moan of his breathing. She touched his hand. It was cool. Hiep moved his foot and turned on his side, the wooden legs of the narrow cot squeaking under his weight.

"Uncle Hiep, can you hear me? It's Mai. Tuan brought you to the clinic. The doctor is taking care of you. You're going to be all right." *Can the doctor's medicine defeat Sang's curse?*

Hiep's eyes met hers, flickered, and then closed. Mai held his hand and traced her finger around his oval nails, remembering how much she cared for him. She had known him all of her life. He had helped her fly her first kite, standing with her on the dike of the rice paddy and sailing the kite's dragon's body high above the mangroves until it shrank into a small blur in the blue. He had let her hold the string and she had felt the wind tugging at the kite, carrying it farther away from her. The wind had blown harder and the string had started to slip from her small hands when he put his larger hand over hers, steadying the kite and calming her fears. They had flown it together, and he had helped her reel it back in.

When it fell from the sky toward the rice paddy, she'd screamed, "Don't let my dragon get wet," and he had laughed and guided it to a dry landing.

Now Mai turned Hiep's hand over to find the lifeline in his palm, hoping that it would foretell a long life. But it stopped in the middle of his palm. *Will his life be short?* She couldn't let that happen. She would have to do something. Covering him carefully with the mosquito netting, Mai left the tent, holding her rocking stomach, afraid she would vomit again.

Where was Tuan? He had promised to bring the tiger pictures back. The tropical sun was setting, the rose-pink glow of twilight spattering the clouds before the night sky would hang its blanket over the island. If she hurried, she could make it back to camp before dark; she could bring the tigers to Hiep early in the morning. But when she turned her tired body toward the south of the island, the rain rang in torrents and the ground, already saturated, became a pool of mud. She spun around and dashed toward the clinic. The water crossing would be impossible in this storm. Where could she go?

Mai collided with a short, familiar figure also rushing through the rain. When she looked up, she saw Kien's face, his mouth wide with surprise.

"Kien, what are you doing here?"

He clasped her hand and guided her toward the clinic. They stepped into its shelter, out of the storm, listening to the pounding on the tarp above them.

"I'm so glad to see you," Mai sobbed, wrapping her arms around her shivering shoulders.

"I came to see how Hiep is," said Kien, the rainwater running in rivulets down his face, his dark hair matted against his neck. "Lan and Kim told me what happened. I was out collecting wood when you left."

"He's very sick. The doctor said he had hepatitis."

Kien reached out to touch Mai's trembling fingers. She pulled them away.

"I need to get back to our tent and get the tiger pictures to protect Uncle Hiep from Sang's ghost. Small Auntie stole my gold bracelet, and now our good luck is gone. If I don't get the tiger pictures, Hiep will die." Mai's voice mingled with the whine of the wind beating against the tent. Just then, the dour-faced nurse appeared from behind the partition.

"What are you doing here? You have to leave." She waved her arms in the air, trying to shoo them out as if they were the mosquitoes that descended at twilight.

"We need to see the doctor. Our friend Hiep is here. We want to find out how he is." Kien took one step toward the nurse while Mai edged behind him.

"The doctor is only here in the mornings. Come back then." She walked toward them and herded them out of the tent, into the wet night, pulling the flap down after them.

"Come on, Mai, let's go to the food tent." Kien grabbed Mai's hand and pulled her after him, dashing toward a canvas enclosure across the beach where she could see a welcoming light flickering. Mai stumbled into the tent, still gripping Kien's hand, relieved to be out of the storm. Several long wooden tables stood in the shadows, which she knew would remain empty until the ship loaded with food arrived from the mainland in the morning. A small lantern flickered in the center of one table, but no one was there. Kien and Mai huddled together in a dry, dark corner where Mai hoped they would not be discovered. She brushed the water from her face.

She could hear the squish of Kien's T-shirt as he removed it and wrung it out. She wished that she were a boy so she could do the same, but her nipples had started to turn into large bumps like mosquito bites and she was embarrassed.

She remembered how upset she'd been when she'd started to bleed. She had felt a wetness between her legs one morning shortly after she'd arrived on the island. Her stomach had begun to cramp. She'd slid her hand into her pants and felt a sticky substance high on her thigh. Blood. If only her mother were here. She had gone to Small Auntie.

"Am I going to die?" she'd asked.

Small Auntie smiled. "No, Mai. No dying. You've just started your *kinh*, your monthly bleeding. You're a woman now."

"But I don't want to be. Why must I bleed?"

"Some day you will have babies." Small Auntie had showed her how to tie a rice bag cloth between her legs. Now, being around Lan and Kim and the other older girls, she had begun to understand and accept what was happening to her body. They'd laughed when she had hunched her shoulders so that her breasts wouldn't show.

"It's all right, Mai. Stand up. Be proud to be a woman," Lan said. She smiled back at her, but around Kien she was self-conscious of her budding body.

Mai shivered in her soaked clothing, listening to the rain beating the tarp above them. Her finger traced the long scratch that Small Auntie's nail had carved on her stomach. She could feel the blood crusted in its crevice.

"Kien, I'm worried about Uncle Hiep. Do you think he'll be all right? I want to go see him first thing in the morning."

"Of course. We'll hang out by the pier and wait for the doctor to come from the mainland."

"Tuan went to get the tiger pictures. I hope he gets back before it's too late," Mai said.

"Shh. I think I hear someone," Kien whispered, touching her arm.

Two figures silhouetted by the faint light of the lantern ducked in the tent. Just then the wick of the lantern sputtered and the flame went out. Mai reached for Kien, pressing her nails into his arm. She could hear the sound of a match being struck and see the faces of two Malaysian soldiers as they lit their cigarettes. The smell of tobacco permeated the dankness of the tent.

After dark, when the Americans and Europeans left the island, the soldiers preyed upon the refugees, stealing from them, hitting them, and raping the women. Lan had warned her to run if she saw a soldier coming. Mai prayed she and Kien would not be discovered. The soldiers moved toward the center of the tent as they laughed and inhaled their cigarettes. Mai and Kien drew farther back into the corner. Mai could hear a steady stream of Malaysian words, but she did not know what they meant. The two lit cigarettes glowed in the darkness like fireflies on a summer's evening.

What if the soldiers stay until daylight? She and Kien had to get out of the tent before they were discovered. She was afraid to think what might happen to them. Just then she heard the voice of a third soldier, and listened as the first two soldiers coughed, grumbled, and followed the third soldier out of the tent and into the rain.

She exhaled in relief. "Do you think they'll come back?"

"I hope not. It's raining pretty hard."

"Where can we go?"

"We'd better just stay here, Mai. It's safer than stumbling around in the dark." Kien reached out and put his arm around Mai. She nuzzled closer, feeling the warmth of his body against hers.

"Remember the monsoons in Vietnam, Kien? I loved to lie in bed and listen to the rain on our tile roof. I felt so safe then." *And,* she thought, *I feel safe with you now.*

"I know what you mean. Weren't you ever afraid?"

Her cheek rubbed against Kien's bare shoulder. She sat very still. "Oh, yes, when the thunder boomed and the lightning made the sky show up like fireworks at Tet, I would hide on the floor next to my bed and call for my nanny."

"My mother and I lived in a bamboo house with a thatched roof that leaked so much when the rain fell, we had to hide under the table. Sometimes the wind would be so fierce I'd have to hold the door shut," Kien said, shivering.

"Well, this isn't much better." Mai laughed as the tarp started to leak above them. They crawled over underneath one of the tables. "I think it's raining more inside now than it is outside."

"Just like home," Kien whispered. "Let's try to get some sleep."

"Kien, can I just ask you a question?"

"Sure, Mai. What is it?"

"Do you think Uncle Hiep is going to be all right?"

Kien did not answer her right away. Maybe he hadn't heard her.

"Do you think Uncle Hiep's going to be all right?" She started to cry.

"Don't cry, Mai. I hope he will be, but I don't know. A friend of my mother's had hepatitis and she recovered."

"But, Kien, Sang's ghost is after Uncle Hiep."

"I believe you, Mai. We'll get those pictures as soon as we can."

Kien's words gave her no peace, and for the rest of the night she lay under the table, listening to Kien's quiet snores and the rain. *Uncle Hiep has to live. He just has to.* She closed her eyes, but sleep was a stranger.

She heard a cough. She scratched her nose and looked over at Kien, who was staring at her.

"Come on, Mai. We need to get out of here now, before someone comes."

As they stepped outside, she felt the first rays of the morning sun on her face. Smoke from cooking fires was curling into the morning mist. She could hear the cry of a hungry baby and see women spreading wet blankets and clothing on rocks and bushes for the sun to dry them. Kien rubbed his chest and unrolled his wet T-shirt. A little girl, her thumb in her mouth, wailed for her mother to pick her up. Mai's stomach started to growl. Kien heard it and laughed. She turned to him and smiled.

"Your stomach is talking to you. Listen to mine. It's talking too." Kien put his hand to his stomach as it too made a gurgling growl. "We'll have to eat when we get back to our camp."

"I want to go see Uncle Hiep first. Then get the tiger pictures," Mai called as she ran across the sand.

Kien sprinted to catch up with her. They crossed the beach by the pier, the wind blowing in their faces. Their open mouths gulped in the sea air. Their feet, dodging debris scattered on the beach by the storm, made deep prints in the wet sand. Mai felt like the kite she'd flown with Hiep, the wind ready to pick her up and blow her into the sky until she became only a small insignificant speck on the horizon.

The American doctor had just stepped off the pier and was striding across the sand toward them. The wooden fishing trawler he'd arrived on bobbed in the waves. Unloading crates containing the morning's food supply were two Malaysians, their bare backs glistening in the sun.

"Doctor, doctor, wait," Mai cried. He veered away from them. Mai and Kien followed him to the clinic, catching up with him as he stooped to empty a stone from his sandal. The doctor slipped his sandal back on and stood up. Mai had forgotten how tall he was.

"I thought I heard someone calling me." He brushed the beads of sweat from his forehead and adjusted the Red Cross cap on his head.

Mai bowed, folding her hands in front of her. "Doctor, please. How is my uncle?"

"Let's go in and see." The doctor motioned her to follow him to the cot where Hiep lay sleeping and pulled back the mosquito netting. The rustle of the mosquito netting moving off his body wakened Hiep, and he opened his eyelids.

"How are you feeling this morning?" the doctor asked as he pressed his fingers to Hiep's wrist. The nurse hovered behind him. Hiep groaned and moved his hand to his side. The doctor reached down and felt it. Hiep groaned louder. Turning to Mai, the doctor said, "He seems to be about the same today. We'll keep an eye on him. You're welcome to come back and check on him any time."

"Thank you, doctor. I'll be back. I have something important to do." Mai squeezed Hiep's hand. "I'll be back in a few hours, Hiep. Don't worry. You're going to be all right."

Hiep's eyes widened as he heard her words. Mai knew she had to get the tiger pictures soon. He wasn't getting better.

When Mai and Kien arrived at the stretch of ocean that divided the island, they stopped to rest, kneeling in the sand to observe the crossing. Mai could see green algae covering the wet rocks. Today, the water circled in mad swirls around the path they would have to cross. Kien beckoned to Mai to follow him.

Mai's legs shook as she stepped out on the first rock. Hiep's life depended on her getting the tiger pictures. She stepped gingerly across the rocks, each one slipperier than the last, holding her dép in her hands and clinging to the rocks with her toes like the monkeys she had seen in the zoo, the salty water sloshing over her feet.

Halfway across she looked back and panicked. She was stranded in the middle. Too late to turn back. She pressed forward until she landed on the last rock, broad and flat, and whispered a silent thank you to the gods who'd protected her despite the fact that she had lost her lucky gold bracelet. The last leap was a small one and she made it easily, sprawling into the sand. She jumped up and grinned triumphantly at Kien.

"I did it," she cried, shading her eyes to look for the tarps. Drawing closer, she could see Lan knitting in the shade of a bamboo tree.

Lan dropped her needles, stood up, and waved. "Mai, how's Hiep? I've been so worried."

"He's very sick. I have to get the tiger pictures. Small Auntie stole my gold bracelet."

"Sit down and have some water and tell me what the doctor said," Lan pleaded, motioning to the water bucket.

Kien dropped to the ground and wiped the perspiration from his forehead. Mai gulped down a can of water and ran into the tent. Over the hammocks were the tiger pictures hanging where she had left them, but now on wet, ripped paper that was covered with black smudges.

"What happened to my pictures?" Mai wailed as she took them down and held them in her hands.

She looked up at Kien as he entered, followed by Lan. Had Sang's ghost destroyed the pictures? What would happen to Hiep now? Mai's body shook with fear.

Lan took one picture from her, examined it, and handed it back to her. "The rain, Mai. It came sideways. There was no way to keep it out. We tried hanging rice bags, but they were not strong enough."

Mai crushed the soggy paper into a ball. Suddenly, she remembered Tuan. "Have you seen Tuan? He came back last night to bring the food and get my pictures for me."

Lan shook her head. "I thought he was with you. I didn't follow you when you crossed the water yesterday. I was afraid. I'm sorry."

"He promised to get the tiger pictures." Mai hurled the paper balls at the side of the tent. "Where is he? I should have left him to watch Uncle Hiep instead of sending him off for the pictures. Now what will I do?" She reached for Hiep's plastic bag hanging from the tent pole and pulled out the drenched pad of paper. "Everything's ruined. I can't even make another picture. There must be some way to make Uncle Sang's ghost rest."

Lan removed the pad of paper from her hand. Mai's arms fell to her side and she hung her head in despair.

"We've come all this way and now we won't be able to leave the island," she said.

"How is Hiep? What did the doctor say?' Lan asked again. Mai repeated the doctor's words. Then she told Lan the details about the theft of her bracelet. Lan gasped.

"Small Auntie shouldn't be allowed to get away with this, but of course on this island we can't stop these things from happening. I'm sorry, Mai. I didn't know you had a bracelet."

Mai hadn't wanted anyone to know about the bracelet, but now it was no matter.

"My mother gave it to me when we left. She told me never to let it go. It was our good luck. It was to remember my family, a promise that we would all be together again, and now the promise can't be kept."

Lan nodded sympathetically. "My mother gave me this small ring." She held out her hand and Mai saw an etched gold band on Lan's index finger. "But now I know my mother is dead and we'll never meet again. Here, Mai, I want you to have this." Lan slipped the ring off her finger. "I want to give you my good luck. It might help to save Hiep." Large tears in the corners of Lan's eyes trailed down her cheeks one at a time, as if each were waiting its turn.

"You didn't tell me your mother was dead. When did you find out?"

Lan's face grew taut. "A letter arrived three days ago from my father. She died of malaria two months ago. A neighbor of ours who just arrived carried it to me."

Mai put her arms around Lan and wept. Together the two stood, Mai's head on Lan's shoulder. Mai wondered if her own mother was still alive.

"Keep the ring. It's your good luck, not mine," Mai protested, pulling back and looking up at Lan. But Lan gently placed the ring in Mai's hand.

"I want you to have it, Mai. It would make me very happy. You know that I care very much for you and Hiep," she said, her cheeks turning crimson.

Mai could see that Lan was sincere, but Mai's sorrow for her would not let her accept such a gift. "No, Lan. I can't accept your mother's ring." She took her friend's hand and slid the ring back on her finger.

Lan looked down at her round band and then up at Mai. Her eyes were bright, and her lashes were moist. "I will wear it for your good luck." She gave a half-smile.

Mai took Lan's hand. "Thank you from the bottom of my heart. I've never had such a wonderful gift offered to me. But now that my bracelet is gone, I think I will have to make my own good luck."

Fifteen

Mai had to get back to Hiep. The rain had started to flood the island again and she was worried that she wouldn't be able to cross the water. It had been foolish to come all this way for the tiger pictures. Tuan, no doubt, had realized that and stayed near the clinic last night. She needed to find him too. By now sheets of rain were slicing through the tent, the tarp on top flapping against the tent poles it was tied to, fighting to get loose and fly away.

"Over here." Lan beckoned to a spot in a corner, where several empty rice bags had been lashed to the ground. They huddled together as the rain ran in rivulets through the tent. The storm raged all day and into the night. Mai curled up in her hammock and worried about Hiep.

"Can't we try the crossing? I'm so worried about Uncle Hiep," Mai called to Kien, who was lying in his hammock.

"You'll drown if you try to cross in this," he warned, and she realized he was right.

How she wished her father were here. He would know what to do. But he wasn't, and it was up to her. She felt old, older than she wanted to feel.

How she longed to be a child again, climbing the trees in the orchard behind the house with her cousins and the servants' children, sitting in the shade sipping a bottle of sweet sugar-cane drink, hearing the clatter of her sandals as she skipped along the tile path that ran the length of their house. Eating her favorite food, *bun thit nuong:* grilled pork with white rice noodles. Her stomach moaned, even though Lan had fed her two bowls of cold rice and vegetables before bedtime.

"Kien, are you still awake?"

"Yes, Mai, I can't sleep."

"Neither can I. I keep thinking about Uncle Hiep and Sang's ghost. I'm afraid he's working his evil on Hiep and that he's going to make him die."

"The doctor will help Hiep, Mai. His medicine is stronger than Sang's ghost."

"I hope so, Kien. We were so happy before we lost the war, before all of this. I just hope our family can all be together again. I think the evil spirits are winning." Mai sat up in the dark, on the wooden bench that was now her bed.

"Mai, you know you can count on me to help you. I'll help you fight Sang's ghost. He won't be able to win."

Mai heard the strength in Kien's voice and it comforted her.

"You know, Kien, he hasn't visited me since we took Uncle Hiep to the clinic. I hope he isn't bothering Hiep. He's all alone there."

Kien's face never left Mai as she watched the constant rain pound the beach the next day. No trips were made to the main camp. Mai could hear the rip of the metal when Lan opened two cans of beef stew. A little rice lay in a bag out of the rain, but it was impossible to build a fire. Mai could smell the strong aroma of the beef wafting across the tent and her stomach jumped. They had been conserving their food for the last few days. If the rain didn't stop, Mai did not know what they would do. She lay in her hammock worrying about Hiep.

She glanced at her English composition book, then picked up her knitting needles and examined the scarf she was working on. The stitches were uneven and the surface was lumpy, but she was pleased with her first attempt at making an article of clothing. Mother would be so proud of her, and Grandmother would cluck her teeth and say, "Maybe that girl isn't as lazy as I thought she was." Grandmother was always scolding her for playing too much or not being clean enough. She didn't believe that children should be children.

Mai tried to distract herself, but she saw Hiep's face dancing before her—his yellow eyes, his parched lips, and his hollow cheeks. She wrapped the scarf around her neck, careful not to poke herself with the knitting needles. It needed to be a little longer, she thought. Those winters were going to be very cold.

Winter. Will I ever see it? Will Uncle Hiep ever see it? When Father had described America, it had sounded like a dream come true. But after living on the island for a while, enough reports had come back from resettled refugees about the harsh realities of their new life that Mai had become afraid of what the future might bring. For her and most of the young educated Chinese people who lived on the south of the island, life had been one of privilege and of power. All that had been taken away when the Communists came, and she didn't know what would become of her.

In America, she had heard, the government changed every four years so that the same people didn't stay in control all of the time. *What kind of place can it be?* Her stomach tightened with fear when she thought of it. She did not want her father to find out that life in America would be hard. It felt strange to suddenly feel protective of him. He had always been the protector, which was why everyone in the village looked up to him and went to him for help. It would be difficult for her family to start over, but at least they would be together.

"Mai, come and eat," Lan called. "I'm sorry it's not warm. It's too wet to build a fire."

Mai put two spoonfuls of stew on her tin plate, clinking her spoon against the can.

"Take more," Lan urged.

Mai shook her head, her eyes lowered. "I know this is almost the end of the food. Someone has got to go to the main camp." She licked her lips, savoring the taste of meat and gravy.

"It's too dangerous, Mai. We could drown." Lan put the can down.

"I'm tired of waiting. I need to see Uncle Hiep and find out how he is, and we need more food."

"If Tuan is with him, he'll be taken care of. The best thing to do is wait."

"I can't wait. Uncle Hiep's life is in danger." Mai smashed

a mosquito as it landed on her arm and flicked it to the ground.

Just then Kien came dripping into the tent. "Quick. You won't believe your eyes." He pointed to the sea.

"What is it, Kien?" Mai jumped to her feet and clutched his arm.

"A trawler. They've sent supplies." Kien clapped his hands and jumped in the air.

Mai's chopsticks clattered against her tin plate as she pushed the hanging rice bags aside and rushed down to the shore. A fishing trawler, its deck stacked high with wooden boxes, chugged slowly through the water about two hundred feet from shore. Mai stood and watched as it moved across the water.

"Stop," she cried. She waved to three Malaysian sailors who stood on the deck, but they looked straight ahead as the trawler disappeared around the edge of the island. Kien stood by her side, his mouth open.

"Why didn't they stop? Don't they know we need food?" Mai complained.

"I guess there's no place to come in here without hitting the reefs. The boxes of food would just sink if they threw them into the waves. I'm sorry I got our hopes up," Kien said, turning to walk back to the tent.

Mai followed, wondering what she should do now. There was no way she could help Hiep while she was trapped here. Or was there?

Sang's body still lay at the bottom of the well, despite his spirit wandering, seeking vengeance. She remembered her parents taking food and paper money and clothing to funerals to present to the dead to use in the afterlife. She didn't have any paper money or clothing, but she could take some food to the well to appease Sang's ghost. She would have to do it secretly, for they had so little food left she was sure no one would let her take some to feed a ghost when so many living people would be starving soon. But perhaps Sang would leave them alone and let Hiep live.

She would have to find some food. *Can I do it?* The food would be the easiest part of the plan. Taking it to the well was frightening. Everyone knew the well was haunted now. *Can I face Sang's ghost?*

If only there was someone who would go with her. She knew Lan and Kim wouldn't go. When they had heard of Small Auntie's threats, they had warned her to stay away from the well. No, she would do this by herself.

That evening, as she divided the last can of chicken curry with Lan and Kien, Mai waited until no one was looking and hid her portion in a tin can, covering it with the plastic bag. The rain that had drenched the island all day ceased after dinner, and Kien and Lan went to check the crossing.

Mai perched on a rock with Kim, knitting her scarf, waiting for the sun to set so she could steal off to the well. It wasn't far from camp, but she knew if she told anyone what she was doing, they'd stop her. She could hear them now, chastising her for wasting good food. But she had to save Hiep, and with the tiger pictures gone, it was her only chance.

Kien and Lan stopped by the fire. Mai looked up at Kien.

"The water is down a little. If it doesn't rain any more, we should be able to cross by morning." Kien's shoulders tightened. "It will still be very dangerous."

"But what if it isn't down? What will we do?" Mai couldn't believe that they would be left to starve.

"Don't worry, Mai. We'll get across. We just have to time it." Kien's voice was confident, but his solemn expression betrayed him. Mai followed him toward the tent.

"Kien, can I talk to you?" She hadn't planned on confiding in him, but she needed to know what he thought. She realized that she was too frightened to go to the well by herself.

"Of course, Mai. What is it?" He took a step toward her and looked into her eyes.

"I have to ask you about something. But it's private. Can we walk down by the shore and talk?"

He nodded and turned toward the beach, and she walked by his side, trying to decide where to begin. The full moon cast a silver path across the dark water, its beams dancing on the crests of the waves. The brinish smell of the sea stung her nostrils. She could hear Kien's soft breathing and the padding of his feet through the sand. The blood rushed through her as his arm brushed hers. What would he think of her plan? Would he laugh? They walked along in silence for a while, listening to the murmurs of voices from the camp mingled with the ripple of the ebbing and flowing of the waves.

"Do you ever wish you had never left home, Mai?" Kien's hands were stuck in his pockets. His eyes searched the black horizon.

"What do you mean, Kien?"

"I mean, do you wish you had stayed with your family, no matter what happened?"

"I don't know. I don't really feel I had a choice."

"But what if you never see your family again?" Kien stopped and kicked a broken shell with his bare foot. "Sometimes I feel like I'm all alone in the world."

"I know how you feel, but you're not alone, Kien. You have me." Embarrassed, Mai quickly corrected herself. "I mean, us—Lan, Kim, Tuan, everyone."

"I'm glad you're here, Mai. I don't feel so alone." Kien took her hand. "You're my best friend. I've never had a best friend before."

Mai didn't know what to say. She had never had a friendship with anyone outside her family, certainly not a boy, but she felt more than friendship for him. She had never been encouraged to express her feelings and so she kept them to herself, squeezing his hand as it encircled hers.

"Kien," she stammered, "I've got another plan to stop Sang's ghost from killing Hiep. Will you help me?"

Kien arched his eyes in surprise. "What do you want to do?"

Mai explained her plan to take the food to the well and present it to Sang's ghost to enjoy in the afterlife, appeasing him so that he would not seek vengeance for his death.

"I've got to go tonight, Kien. I've hidden some food in my hammock. Will you go with me? His ghost may be at the well, and I'm not sure what he will do when he sees me."

"We'll have to go early. Lan and I are going to check the crossing around midnight to see if the water is down. I've got a little extra food too. I'll bring it."

Mai balled her fists into the bottom of her blouse. "I'll wait until everyone has gone to their hammocks. Then we'll slip out."

Kien nodded and touched her on the cheek. "You're a very brave girl to confront a ghost. Are you sure you want to do this?"

"If you don't want to go, just say so." Mai pulled away from Kien.

"Now wait a minute. Don't get angry. You know I'll help you. It's just that…"

"You don't believe me, do you? You think I'm some silly superstitious girl from the village. Well, I will have to go by myself if you won't come." Mai turned her back to Kien.

Kien grabbed Mai's shoulder and spun her around, his blue eyes narrowing, his cheeks drawn taut.

"I do believe in ghosts. I have my own."

"What do you mean?" Mai's voice softened.

"I never told you about what happened to me before I arrived on this island."

"You can tell me, Kien. I want to know all about you."

"I made a decision that I would never tell anyone. But I want *you* to know." Kien sat on the ground and Mai sat down beside him.

"When I was on the boat, we were attacked by Thai pirates. They killed most of the men and took our boat. They left the rest of us on a very small island. There was nothing to eat, and everyone was starving." Kien's eyes became wet with tears. "At first, I didn't understand what was happening. When I was asleep, my friend Duc disappeared. When I asked where he was, no one seemed to know. It was as if he had vanished into thin air. That day we had a delicious stew that I was told came from a boar that had been killed. I believed them, but the island was so small, there were no animals. Finally, as more people—all of them single people traveling by themselves without family— disappeared, I discovered what was happening. An old woman told me, 'Watch out. Sleep with your eyes open. You are next.' I asked her what she meant, and she just cackled. But that night I had a dream, and in the dream I saw the ghosts of all the people who had disappeared, warning me to be careful. Then I knew. We had been eating them. I was next—the last single person, with no family, no one to defend me."

Mai gasped. "What did you do?"

"At first I didn't believe her. But then I realized there was nothing I could do. There was no place to hide and no one to defend me. I was so sickened by what she had told me that I didn't care if I lived or died. But the next morning a ship stopped, rescued us, and brought us inside the Malaysian waters. It dropped us off here."

"But what about the people who were with you? Are they on this island?"

"Yes. That's why I moved down here right away. I was afraid they would try to keep me from talking about what they did. But I was a part of it. I have trouble sleeping. The ghosts of those people haunt me."

"How many were there?" Mai's stomach rolled.

"They killed four people. My friend Duc, two young girls, and a teenage boy." Kien's voice dropped to a whisper and his lips barely moved, as if the words were stuck in his throat.

"You have to tell someone. What they did was wrong." Mai's whole body shook, but she felt sorry for Kien instead of repulsed at what he had done.

"If they hadn't done what they did, we would all be dead. We were on that island for several weeks. I'm just glad we were rescued before they killed me."

"I'm sorry I doubted you. Thank you for telling me. Your secret is safe." Mai tried to keep her voice steady. She had heard of the cruelty of the Thai pirates, the rapes, the murders, but not this. How could you eat another human being?

The Vietnamese on the island helped each other, shared their food if someone was hungry, offered shelter to those without it, and banded together to protect each other from the harsh treatment of the Malaysian soldiers. All except Small Auntie, of course. But even she had offered them shelter. Mai looked at Kien, sitting with his head in his hands, and wanted to put her arms around him as Ba Du had done with her. She stood up and cleared her throat.

"Kien, the others have all gone in now. Do you still feel like helping me? It's all right if you don't want to."

Kien looked up. "I want to help you. Thanks for listening. I feel as if a bag of stones has been removed from my body."

Mai slipped back into the tent, through the rice bag partitions, and took the small can of food she had hidden. She dropped it in her plastic bag and walked outside, where Kien was waiting. A few people were milling around on the beach, but most were under mosquito nets in their hammocks. Mai and Kien hurried along the edge of the jungle until they came to a place where the foliage was trampled.

"It's a good thing the moon is out tonight. The well is back through these trees, along this path," Mai said.

A shrill sound came from the treetop. A wail like a soul in agony. Mai froze. Sang's ghost. Had he seen them?

"Quick, Kien. Run. It's his ghost. He knows we're here."

They ducked into the jungle and flattened their bodies under a low lying fern.

"Mai, I think that was a bird. I've heard that sound before, early in the morning when I've gone out for sea cucumbers. Don't be afraid," Kien whispered as he lay prone on the ground beside her.

Mai could smell the scent of the soil in her nostrils and feel the cool dampness of the undergrowth against her skin. She lifted her head and looked toward the treetops at a flutter of wings silhouetted against the moonlit sky. Another melancholy wail pierced the night's stillness, and then diminished as the wings dissolved into the darkness.

Feeling foolish and relieved, she and Kien stood up and pushed their way through the undergrowth to a path that led them along the edge of the jungle. A large clearing appeared, where a bare circular patch of ground lay partially covered by green vines. A small pile of rocks next to the circle bore testimony to the failed attempt to rescue Sang.

Mai looked at the covered well. Deep beneath that circle lay Sang's body, probably already becoming one with the soil. She motioned to Kien and they moved one step at a time across the small space. Mai pulled out her can of food. She knelt on her knees, placed the food on the well site, and bowed to the earth. Kien did the same, and then they folded their hands over their hearts and chanted a prayer for the dead, their monotone song echoing in the darkness.

They remained prone after their chant, Mai praying silently for the release of Sang's spirit to the afterworld. A branch cracked behind them and, startled, they jumped to their feet. They covered the food with vines and hid in the bushes.

A faint glow of morning light seeped through the trees. Had they been there all night? What would the others say?

Kien was not upset. He told her that he and Lan had decided not to check the water until morning, when they would be able to cross in the light. Mai felt triumphant, sure they had satisfied the ghost with their offerings.

"Now he can rest. His soul can go to the afterworld and won't have to wander anymore," Mai said. *And Hiep will be safe*, she thought to herself.

"We'd better get back. The others will wonder where we were," said Kien.

Mai trotted behind him, anxious to eat breakfast but knowing there might not be any. The food had run out, unless Lan had found more. "Kien, let's go back to camp separately," she said.

"Don't worry, Mai. You go first. I'll come later and pretend I went out early to check the water."

Mai slipped back into the tent and saw that Lan's hammock was empty. No one was around. A few minutes later, Kien entered.

"Where has everyone gone?" he asked.

"I don't know," Mai replied. "You don't think they've all gone to the main camp to get food, do you?"

"Perhaps. The water must have gone down. Let's go see."

Mai was anxious to see Hiep and eat. It would be good to get to the main camp.

"Do you feel better about Sang's ghost, Mai?" Kien asked.

"I hope it worked, but I'm anxious to see Uncle Hiep."

Sixteen

Mai saw footprints in the sand when they reached the crossing. The water level was low, and the sun had broken through the cloudy sky. A rainbow was arching its way across the horizon as if its brilliant hues had been placed there by a giant paintbrush. They crossed the water without incident, and hurried on to the main camp, where a line of people holding hands were wading into the sea. The supply ship was anchored far out because the wooden pier had been damaged by the storms. Mai spotted Lan and Kim in the middle of the chain.

"Come on, we'll have to go out too if we want to get our food." Kien extended his hand to Mai and wading out in the water toward Kim and Lan.

A large wave lifted Mai off her feet, and she tried to hold on to Kien's hand as the force of the wave pushed her under, dashing her against the coral. She gasped as she swallowed the salty sea, struggling to get her head to the surface. She couldn't drown. She had to get to Hiep to see if he was all right, to make sure Sang's ghost had been satisfied. Another wave washed over her, lifting her to her feet, and she moved her arms and kicked her feet, trying to swim out to the ship. A hand gripped her shoulder and pulled her up and she saw Kien, his shoulders popping out of the water, his feet cycling in the water.

"Hold on to me and swim," he called, and together they kicked and swam out to the ship, where a pot-bellied Malaysian with a heart tattoo on his chest was tossing food into the water. Mai saw Lan swim up and try to catch a loaf of bread that flew over her head, landing in the water. A gray-headed man behind her grabbed it and handed it to Lan. Kim caught the bag of rice that came soaring through the air when she called her name to the sailor.

"Nguyen Mai, two people," called Mai, then paddled up to catch her loaf of bread. A small bag of rice landed in front of her and she grabbed it before it disappeared beneath the surface. Then she turned to swim back to shore, where dozens of drenched swimmers were struggling out of the water with their bags of rice and loaves of bread.

Where had Kien gone? She could see Lan and Kim waving to her, but not Kien. She swam toward the beach, and as her feet touched the sand, she looked up and there he was, holding a bag of rice high above his head. They collapsed on the edge of the beach gazing at each other. Kien smiled and squeezed the bag of rice.

"Finally, something to eat. Are you as hungry as I am?" he asked, pulling off a hunk of bread from his loaf and offering it to her.

"Eat it, I have my own," she said.

Kien stuffed a piece of bread in his mouth and wrinkled

up his nose. "Ugh, it tastes bad. The sea water has made it soggy."

Mai offered him a piece of hers. He shook his head. "That's yours. I shouldn't be so picky. There were many times in our village when we only had one bowl of rice a day. My mother often gave me her food and went hungry. I would ask her if she was going to eat, and she would smile and say she already had."

Mai jumped up and looked around.

"What's the matter, Mai? What are you looking at?"

"I've got to go see how my uncle is." Mai picked up the rice and bread and turned to look at Kien.

"Wait." Kien stuffed another bite of bread into his mouth, made a face, and stood up. Mai could see the profile of the doctor standing in the doorway of the clinic, talking to a short woman with an infant in her arms. Mai squirmed while he finished talking to the woman, then walked across the sand to him.

"Doctor, could I speak to you?"

"What is it? Oh, yes, I remember you."

"My uncle, how is he?"

The doctor folded his hands. "We had to send him to the hospital on the mainland. He started to have convulsions."

"How is he now? Can I go to the mainland to see him?"

"No, that's not possible."

"Is he going to be all right? He's the only family I have here." *Why did I leave him?*

"Please come inside and sit down." The doctor motioned to her. Mai followed him into the clinic and sat on a low bench while Kien waited outside. She searched the doctor's face. Hiep was all right, she was certain. Sang's ghost had been appeased. She had made sure of that.

"I'm afraid I have bad news for you. We did all we could at the hospital, but your uncle took an unexpected turn for the worse."

"What do you mean? Where is he now?" Mai's lips quivered. No, it couldn't be.

The doctor put one hand on the stethoscope around his neck and cleared his throat. "Your uncle died yesterday morning. I'm very sorry."

"No, no, you said he would be all right. Remember? You gave him the shot." Mai started to sob. She had failed. The ghost had won.

"Sometimes the shot doesn't work. We've had many people die from hepatitis." The doctor looked around uneasily. "Is that your friend with you?"

Mai nodded her head between sobs. The doctor walked over to the entrance of the tent and said something to Kien. He nodded solemnly and walked over to Mai and touched her hair. The doctor continued. "As I said, we did our best."

Mai peered up at the doctor through her tears and several strands of hair that fell across her eyes.

"I want to see him. I want to give him a proper burial," she said, her arms folded across her chest. She thought of Hiep, alone, dying, and felt as if she would die too.

"He's already been buried in the cemetery on the mainland. We didn't know where you were." The doctor sounded as if he had spent enough time with her and wanted to go.

"We were trapped on the south end of the island. We just got here." Mai kept sobbing.

"Come on, Mai. There's nothing we can do now." Kien picked up Mai's rice and bread, which she'd dropped at her feet, and touched her hand. Mai followed him, her feet moving as if they were made of wood. They sat down under a palm tree and Mai stopped crying.

"I was too late. Sang's ghost had already punished him before I even got to the well. It's all my fault. I should have gone there sooner. Small Auntie would not let Sang be appeased. She made him kill Hiep. That's why she took my gold bracelet. It was our good fortune and it was protecting Hiep. I should have gotten the gold bracelet back."

"Mai, it's not your fault. Just like Sang's death was not Hiep's fault. I'm so sorry your uncle died."

Kien was trying to comfort her, but she didn't want to be comforted. She was angry and she was afraid. If Sang's ghost had been able to kill Hiep, what was going to happen to her? She needed to get her gold bracelet back from Small Auntie before anything else happened.

A voice blaring from the loudspeaker in Vietnamese broke through her thoughts. "The following people please report immediately to the Red Cross tent for immigration." A list of names followed. Perhaps today would be the day her name would be called. She tilted her head toward the loudspeaker. Twenty names shot out of the metal horn. Hers was not among them, but Small Auntie's was. How could this be? She had to get the bracelet back.

"I'll meet you back at camp," she said to Kien. He looked at her in surprise. "I have something I need to do. You go on."

Shrugging his shoulders, he headed off. Mai raced to the Red Cross tent and almost stepped on a small boy sitting cross-legged in the sand.

"Oh, I'm sorry," she said. She looked down and saw the somber face of Minh.

Mai's first impulse was to grab Minh and demand he take her to Small Auntie, but her anger at Small Auntie was temporarily forgotten in her joy at seeing Minh again. Since that day at the market when he'd told her he was not allowed to talk to her, she'd only glimpsed him from a distance. She missed the way he used to skip ahead of her when they went looking for firewood and the funny little smile he gave when he thought she wasn't looking.

Minh scowled when he recognized her. He started to move away from her, but she put her hand on his shoulder.

"Don't go, Minh. Please." Mai was surprised at the tears that welled up in his eyes when he turned to look at her. "What's the matter, Minh? Why are you unhappy? I just heard your name called. You're leaving, getting out of here."

Minh wiped the tears trickling down his cheeks with the backs of his dirt-streaked hands. "I don't want to go without my father. I'm afraid."

Mai felt sad and guilty at the same time. She had been so worried about Hiep that she hadn't realized what effect Sang's death might have on his children. How would his family survive in a strange country without him? How would they find a place to live? Would Minh be able to go to school or, as the oldest son, would he have to find a job support them? Who would protect them? She thought of her own fears and the thought of going to America without her uncle. She hoped Third Uncle in Chicago would still want her. But could she make the journey across another ocean by herself? She was alone now too.

"Don't be afraid, Minh. I've heard that America is a wonderful place. They give you a place to live and food to eat. You won't starve. And you can go to school for free." Mai especially liked hearing that school was free. How she missed school.

Minh stopped rubbing his eyes. The look on his small round face told her that he didn't believe her.

"It's true," she said.

"I don't care about school. I want my father." Minh shoved his hands in his pockets, biting his lower lip. "Mother says it's your uncle's fault he's dead."

Mai shook her head. "Uncle Hiep is dead now. I think your father's ghost killed him."

Minh's mouth dropped open.

"My father's ghost. What do you mean?"

"Your father's ghost has been haunting us. I thought I had made peace with him, but when I returned to the clinic, my uncle had died of hepatitis."

"But how could my father be a ghost?" Minh's eyes grew as round as the coconuts that hung on the palm trees above them. "My father wouldn't kill anyone. Your uncle was the bad man."

Mai sighed. She knew that she could not argue with Minh. He missed his father just as she missed hers. "Where is your mother? I need to see her."

Minh studied the hangnail on his thumb and didn't answer. Mai clenched her teeth and waited for his reply. She was not afraid of Small Auntie anymore, or Sang's ghost. The worst had happened. Hiep was dead. Her only chance now was to get the bracelet back.

"Did you hear me, Minh? It's very important that I find her." Mai's bangs slid down her forehead.

"She's in there. We have to see the doctor before we can leave."

Minh pointed to an opening in the tent. Mai walked over and peeked in. A bald man who was slouched at a small table stopped writing and peered up at her over large wire-rimmed glasses perched on his broad nose. That face. He looked like Third Uncle. But, of course, he wasn't. Third Uncle was in Chicago waiting for her to come. Third Uncle was much younger.

"What do you want?" the man asked in Vietnamese, his open mouth revealing several gaps where teeth had once lodged. Mai shook her head and backed out.

Minh stood with one hand in his pocket, glaring at her. "My mother should be out in a minute, but I don't think she wants to see you."

"Minh, I don't know how to tell you this. My gold bracelet. Your mother stole it from me. I want it back." Mai kicked sand into the air with her toe.

Minh frowned and pulled his hand out of his pocket. In his palm he cradled a thin bracelet, finely tooled with delicate flowers and round as a pomegranate, its color a deep burnished gold.

"Is this it? Mother asked me to guard it while she saw the doctor."

Mai spoke carefully. "That looks like it. May I see it?"

Minh shrank back and closed his hand around the bracelet. "Mother told me to take good care of it."

"Just let me look at it. Does it have the initials *NL* inside?" The bracelet had been a wedding present to Mai's mother from her father, and he had engraved his initials inside it: *NL*, Nguyen Loi.

Minh hesitated for a moment, then held the bracelet close to his eyes and squinted. "It does," he said. He looked at her, the bracelet shaking in his hands.

"Minh, you have to give it to me. My mother gave it to me for my good fortune. Your mother stole it from me. It will only bring you bad luck."

Minh stuffed the bracelet back in his pocket. "My mother will be very angry if I give you the bracelet." He gave her a cold stare.

"But it's mine. She took it from me. You can't keep it." Mai reached out her hands, palms up, her lips were quivering. "Do you want to have bad fortune? Give it to me and tell your mother you lost it. She'll believe you."

Minh hesitated, peered toward the tent, and then pulled the bracelet back out of his pocket. "Here. I don't want any more bad fortune." He dangled the bracelet in front of Mai, who grabbed it, shoved it in her pocket, and gave him a hug. He shrank back from her.

"Thank you, Minh, thank you," she said. "You've saved both our lives. Don't be afraid to leave the island without your father. He would want you to go. There's no life here. It's just a place to wait for life to begin again. Life will begin."

She said the words to convince herself as much as Minh. Would life begin again for her? She hoped so. She had been on this island for almost half a year, yearning for a new life. When Hiep had heard from another refugee that everyone in America drove a car, his eyes had glowed with excitement.

"I'll drive a Mercedes," he had said, slicking back his hair behind his ears and puffing up his small chest.

She didn't want to have to bear the news to her family of his death. Life had been sad enough. But what would become of her now? She would have to travel to America by herself. If she got to go. She felt the gold bracelet deep in her pocket and rubbed it between her thumb and forefinger for luck. She'd better get away before Small Auntie discovered the bracelet was gone.

"Goodbye, Minh. I hope you have a good life." Tomorrow, or the next day, Minh and his family would be gone on the early boat to the mainland, and then Small Auntie would not be able to take the bracelet away. Mai would have to hide until then.

"Goodbye. Maybe we'll see each other again." A smile crept across the solemn landscape of Minh's face.

The sun splattered over the fine white sand as Mai returned to their camp, her chest heaving. Pushing back the hanging rice bag, she entered the section of the tent that Hiep and she had shared. His hammock hung limply between two poles, a brown plastic bag dangling from one, his few possessions in it.

Mai removed the bag from the hook and opened it. A crumpled white T-shirt and a tan pair of shorts lay on top. Underneath was the shiny metal can opener with the black handle her uncle had traded three cans of peas for at the market, and a deck of cards. How Hiep had loved to gamble. It had taken Mai a while to discover that he went to card games when he stayed out late at night. She hadn't minded. At least he had found something to entertain himself, and he had no money to lose. Sometimes he'd even won extra food for them.

Mai's gaze went over to her hammock. Four small cans for drinking and eating lined the edge of a small bench. Next to them, the oil-filled can Hiep had fashioned into a candle stood by the two halves of a large oil can he had cut for cooking pots.

She reached up and ran her fingers across her red bag. The zipper whined as she opened it and pulled out the red blouse and the pair of black pants. She smoothed the wrinkles in the cotton blouse and thought of the day when she would wear this outfit to America. Mother had sewn them just for that. Underneath the outfit lay her plainer blouse and pants, along with her notebook, pencil, yarn, knitting needles, and the lumpy scarf she'd made. Mai sighed, folded the outfit, and replaced it in the bag. Unfolding and folding her "going to America" clothes had become a morning ritual with her. Sometimes she even slipped them on and pretended she'd heard her name over the loudspeaker.

She stroked the bracelet deep in her pants pocket. When it was dark and no one was around, she would bury it in the sand under her cooking fire. She should have hidden it there when she first came to this camp instead of carrying it tucked in her waistband, but she wanted it close to her so that she could feel its power. Now she wanted to gaze at it, the bracelet she had nearly lost. *Mother, I have not failed you*, she thought.

She edged into a corner of the tent, then slid the bracelet from her pocket and held it to the light with both hands, admiring the deep glow of its burnished gold. She pushed it on her wrist, its power warming her fingertips and sending a rush of heat through her body. Her ears tingled and her knees trembled. *I shall never let you go again*, she promised it. *Mother gave you to me to help me through this journey and I will hold on to you with all my might.* Folding her hands around the bracelet, she prayed to Buddha for strength and wisdom and then solemnly returned the bracelet to the dark folds of her pocket.

When the crimson cast of day kissed the horizon with its last beams of light, Mai listened to the singsong voices gossiping near the water's edge, the cry of a soaring seagull, the creaking of the tent poles, the clang of pots being hung up to dry, the whoosh of a tent flap being lowered, the pattering of feet on the sand, someone snoring in the space next to her, a gentle laugh, and the beating of her own heart. Alive—this was how it felt.

She listened until the voices from the water's edge retreated to their tents, and then she crept over to her cooking fire, three large rocks arranged in a triangle. Reaching down and lifting the ashes from the hole in the center, she dropped them on the sand, then dug a deeper pit within the fire hole. She placed the bracelet, wrapped in a small corner of rice bag, in the hole. The briny dampness invaded her nostrils as she patted the sand over the bracelet and scooped the ashes back in the fire hole. Gleaming beacons on the far-off Malaysian mainland and the blinking lights of a fishing boat on its way to harbor were her only witnesses.

The mainland. That's where they had taken Hiep to die, and then buried him. What it was like, lying in a hole covered by earth? Did he feel anything? Had he known he was going to die? What had he thought about in those last moments? Had he been afraid? Had anyone been with him to hold his hand as his spirit left his body? He had died so far from home. His spirit would not find rest.

She remembered the young woman cast into the deep on her sea journey. The sharks had eaten her. What would happen to Hiep's body? Her parents had never discussed these things in front of her, preferring her to remain innocent and naïve, trying to protect her from life. Now she had to learn on her own.

She crawled back into the tent and stood up, her soul awash with fear and grief. Lighting a tin can candle and placing it on her bench, she tried to focus her eyes in the dim light, but the bamboo tent poles wobbled, her hammock started to sway, and the ground tilted to the sky. The tent rocked like their ship in the stormy sea.

Hold on, hold on, she cried to herself. "Cha, Father, help me." She could see her father's face, with a cigarette drooping from his mouth, exhaling a puff of smoke and smiling at her. She reached out for him, but he was not there. No one was. Kien, where was Kien? "Kien!" Her cries echoed into the darkness.

A soft, petal-like voice called back to her. "Mai, what's the matter?" A hand caressed her aching back with a touch so gentle she thought it might be the wing of a butterfly. She lay on her stomach in her hammock with her eyes closed, afraid to move, afraid the soothing strokes would stop. How wonderful it would be to lie there forever, adrift in this sea of peace. Then the voice spoke again, a voice she knew.

"Don't cry, little one. Whatever it is, I'll help you." Lan, her eyes filled with love, stroked her hair. Mai peered at her through teary lashes.

"Where is Kien? I need him," Mai said, wiping her nose on her sleeve.

"He didn't come back to camp this evening. I don't know where he is. What's wrong?"

"It's Uncle Hiep. They took him to the mainland. He's, he's…" Mai held her head in her hands and started to wail.

"He's what, Mai? Tell me." Lan caught her breath.

"He's dead, Lan. He died. I didn't think he was that sick. If I'd known, I wouldn't have left him." Mai swiped her tears with the tips of her fingers, leaving a dark smudge across her cheekbones. "I just came back to get the tiger pictures so Uncle Sang's ghost wouldn't harm him. And then Kien and I went to the well."

Mai stopped, realizing that the trip to the well was a secret. But what did it matter now? Hiep was dead. Nothing had worked. Sang had won. Her hand froze in midair and then fell limply to her side. She reached for Lan and clutched her in her arms. She could feel the beating of Lan's heart, hear her sobs of anguish as they welled up from deep within her.

Mai began to sob in rhythm with Lan, and together they cried out to the unfair universe that had robbed them of the fair and handsome Hiep. They sat clinging together on the bench, comforting each other with their mournful sounds, as if they were the only two people in the world who had loved Hiep.

Lan *had* loved Hiep. Mai had noticed Lan's shyness around Hiep, and the way she would blush when he spoke to her, but Lan's wails made it clear that her love had been true. Just like in the Chinese operas. The fair maiden dying for love, but in this case, Hiep had died, and Lan, the fair maiden, was left to mourn. Why hadn't Hiep declared his love for Lan? She drew her arms back from Lan and looked at her. Lan, her face damp with tears, lowered her eyes.

"Lan, why didn't you tell me how much you cared for Hiep?"

Lan folded her hands delicately in her lap and did not answer, though a crimson blush crept across her cheeks. Mai thought of Kien and her own love for him. She had not told Lan her secret. Maybe it was better not to tell, but she wanted to share these feelings with someone. Mai enjoyed listening to the girls whisper about their crushes to one another as they sat together in their knitting circle.

She thought of her parents and their marriage. Shuddering, she remembered the time she asked her mother if she had loved her father when they'd gotten married. Her mother, emotionless, had shaken her head.

"My parents arranged the marriage through a matchmaker. Your father's family was very important and very rich," Mother had said, a far-off look in her eyes.

"But they couldn't make you marry him, could they?"

"They were so happy to have me marry him. What could I say?" Mother whispered.

"Was Father handsome? Did he love you?"

"He had good features, but he had only seen me once. We did not marry for love," she sniffed.

"But do you love each other now?" The answer was important to Mai.

"Ours was the largest wedding the village had ever seen. Over three hundred guests."

Mai remembered the framed photograph of her parents on their wedding day, standing in front of the family altar, their hands at their sides, staring at the camera unsmiling, flanked by their friends and parents. Her mother had not answered the question. Mai had not asked it again.

"What's the matter?" Ngoc stepped through the partition, followed by Kim.

Mai's chin trembled, and her voice cracked. "Uncle Hiep's dead."

"It can't be true," Ngoc gulped, grabbing Mai's hand, tears welling in her eyes. She looked over at Lan, who was wiping her tears with her hair. "What happened?"

Mai related the events of the past few days and Ngoc nodded, her jaw dropping in disbelief. Kim shook her head.

"I want him to have a funeral, but the doctor told me he has already been buried," Mai said.

"Did you ask if he had a funeral?" Ngoc replied, pushing a strand of hair out of Mai's eyes.

"No, I didn't think of it. Do you think they might have given him one?"

In a proper Chinese Buddhist funeral like her grandmother's, which Mai remembered, Hiep would have been ushered into the next world by chanting monks and his family's prayers while fake money was burned to ensure that he would not want in the afterlife. When his coffin was lowered into its grave, the mourners would have turned their backs to it and stifled their tears so that his spirit would not wish to remain on earth. Then there would have been forty-nine days of mourning, and visits to the temple once a week to pray for his spirit.

"We could pray for him," Lan said. "I'm sure our ancestors would hear us."

She knelt on the ground and put her palms together. Kim, Ngoc, and Mai knelt down next to her, the sand gritty on Mai's bare knees. Lan chanted softly for Hiep's soul to be received into the afterworld and for it to rest in peace while the three girls followed along, bowing three times before Hiep's hammock, their heads touching the ground each time, their chants seeping through the dangling rice bags and off into the night. Lan's sounds broke off into sobs and she buried her face on the ground. Mai, desolate, stopped and placed her hand on Lan's back.

"Thank you, Lan. I'm sure Uncle Hiep's spirit will be welcomed into the afterlife now." Mai could feel Lan's body calming under her touch. Oh, how she wished Kien were here. Where was he? She needed him now. Lan stood up and hugged Mai.

"We can't do anything else now. He's gone. Go to sleep, Lan. You're tired," Mai said, thinking of the last time she had seen Hiep, lying on that cot in the clinic, his feverish body draped with a mosquito net. How she wished she had stayed with him. She would never forgive herself for leaving him.

"Mai, come and sleep with us. You don't want to be alone tonight," Ngoc said.

"Yes, come with us," Lan urged.

"I'll be all right here. You don't have room for me." Mai wanted to be alone, to grieve by herself, to pray and meditate and ask Buddha to forgive her for neglecting Hiep when he had most needed her, for letting him die alone. Did the girls wonder why she had left him?

"Good night, then," they whispered. "Come get us if you are lonely," Ngoc added as the sisters slipped through the hanging rice bags.

Mai crawled into Hiep's hammock, burying her nose in its mesh, smelling him, his musky odor. What if they had gone to the clinic sooner? If only a Chinese doctor had seen him. Father said Chinese medicine was the most powerful. What kind of medicine did these Americans have? She folded her hands and prayed to Great-grandfather's spirit for release—release from this island, release from her anger—and for forgiveness. An offshore breeze wafted through the tent, gathering her cares in its wings and carrying them out to sea, dropping the seeds of sleep on her as it passed by. Her lids closed, her hands folded in supplication.

A cry pierced the night. Mai covered her ears and wriggled deeper into the folds of her blanket. Another cry followed. She pressed her hands even harder against her ears until the side of her head started to throb from the pressure.

No more ghosts. No more ghosts. Go away and leave me alone, she thought. *I've had enough of you. How many lost spirits roamed the island? So many dead. Away. Away.*

Lifting her hands from her ears, Mai waited for another cry, but all she could hear was the sound of her own breathing. And then she slept.

Seventeen

The next morning Mai poked her head through the opening of Ngoc and Lan's section of the tent. "Did you hear that cry last night?"

Ngoc, her cheeks wrinkled with the lines of sleep, looked up. "No."

It must have been a dream. Was Hiep haunting her now because she had left him?

"Where is Lan?" asked Mai, noticing Lan's empty hammock.

"I don't know. She must have risen before me." Ngoc ran her fingers through her sleep-tousled hair and yawned. Mai slipped on her dép and gathered a pot and a small handful of rice. Little islands of smoke from cooking fires dotted the beach. She approached her fire pit, relieved to see it hadn't been disturbed in the night. Who had cried out? Maybe it had only been a bird. She added a few twigs to the smoldering coals and a flame shot up.

A crackling sound, the woody smell of smoke. A cup of cold water and a handful of rice. She poured these into the cooking pot and balanced it over the fire, scanning the beach for Lan. Where could she be? A voice nagged at Mai: *Go find her.* As soon as the rice had cooked, she decided. The smell made her ravenous; her stomach rumbled. Then she felt a tap on the shoulder. Startled, she turned around. Kien, a bucket of sea cucumbers in his hand, gave her a broad-toothed grin.

"I've brought you a treat for your breakfast," he said, pushing the bucket toward her.

"Kien, I'm so glad to see you. Have you seen Lan? Ngoc and I couldn't find her this morning."

Kien set the bucket on the sand. "She's probably gone for water. Have you checked the well?"

Mai felt foolish as she realized that she and Ngoc hadn't actually searched for Lan. Of course, Lan would be back. But the voice still harped at her. *Go find her.* Could the cry in the night have been Lan's? No, Kim and Ngoc would have heard it, sleeping in the same tent with her.

"It's just that she was so upset about Uncle Hiep. She loved him, you know." Mai lowered her eyes and blushed.

Kien took Mai's hand. "I'll help you find her. You stay here, in case she comes this way, and I'll go to the well."

Mai smiled. "Thank you, Kien. I know I'm probably worrying for nothing."

"I'm sure she's all right." He squeezed her hand and she watched the curve of his back through his T-shirt, the tight muscles in his calves, as he strode down the beach.

One morning a week earlier she and Lan had been sitting on the beach knitting as a Malaysian soldier with a wide grin on his pock-marked face emerged from a thicket of bamboo trees on the edge of the jungle, his long rifle slung over his shoulder, a belt of bullets shining against the dark green of his uniform. The girls cringed and followed him with their lowered eyes. His skin, much darker than theirs, and his eyes, large and deep and separated by a sharp nose, had added to their fright. His fingers fumbled with his belt buckle. Then he'd headed away from them, whistling to himself. Ten minutes later a young girl stumbled onto the beach crying, clutching her shoulders, her dark hair disheveled, her blouse torn.

"What's the matter with her?" Mai had wondered aloud.

Lan had continued to knit, her head down. Mai watched the girl. She fell down in the shallow waves, scrubbing her legs as if trying to wash away a stubborn stain.

"She's a bad girl." Lan pointed her knitting needles at her and pursed her lips.

"Why?" Mai persisted.

"She and that soldier. She did something bad with him."

"What?" Mai dropped her needles in her lap. Silence.

"You don't want to know." Lan turned her face away from Mai so that all she could see was her profile. "That's how girls get extra food. I would rather starve." Lan dropped a stitch and leaned close to her knitting to try to find it.

The girl turned from the waves and lurched her way up the beach to her tent.

"Stay away from girls like that," Lan warned.

Mai had known better than to ask any more questions. The commanding tone of Lan's voice told her this was all of the information she was going to give. Mai had looked up from her knitting out to sea, where a gull dove toward the glassy surface for a fish.

Something was bothering Lan. A sadness had replaced the sparkle in her eyes.

Ngoc came out of the tent, jolting Mai's reverie. "Kien went to the well to find Lan," Mai called.

Ngoc nodded, cupping her chin in her hands. "I thought she would be back by now."

The girls looked at each other, mute. Mai squatted by the fire and stirred the rice. Almost done. She tasted a spoonful, hot on her tongue, the grains soft. Shifting the pot off the fire, she spooned the rice into her tin bowl and sat on her heels, watching the steam rise in the morning air. The rice stuck in her throat. Ngoc knelt beside her. Mai gestured toward the pot. Ngoc shook her head.

"I'm not hungry. I think I'd better go look for Lan. She usually tells me when she's going somewhere."

Mai hesitated. "Did she tell you that she loved Uncle Hiep?"

Ngoc's head jerked around. "She never said a word to me. Why do you say that?"

Mai could hear anger in Ngoc's voice. "I'm sorry. I didn't mean to offend you. I must be mistaken." She looked down at the rice in her chopsticks. Her hands shook and she dropped the rice in the sand. Why was Ngoc angry with her? What was wrong with loving Hiep?

By noon there was still no Lan. Kien and Mai had gone to the middle of the island to collect their rations. Mai had even stopped to ask Miss Cindy if she'd seen Lan. Cindy's blue eyes narrowed in concern. She shook her head. No, she had not seen her.

When they returned, the bags of food over their shoulders, Ngoc was slumped on a rock in the shade of a palm tree, staring at a seashell in her hands.

"Well, was she there?" Ngoc asked, jumping up and running toward them. She stumbled on a branch in the ground and fell on her face at their feet. The shell skittered across the sand. Kien leaned over to help her up, but she pushed his hand away and stood up by herself. Drops of perspiration covered her face and her thick black hair fell over her eyes. She leaned over and retrieved the shell.

"We couldn't find her," Kien answered.

They unpacked the canned goods from the bags, stacked them in the tent on the bench, and then joined Kim in the shade of a palm eating leftover rice from breakfast. "She'll be back by dinner, wherever she is. Don't worry," said Kien, brushing a fly from his bowl of rice.

But the sun began its afternoon descent toward the horizon and Lan did not return.

"We should have checked the clinic. Do you think she's sick and didn't tell us?" Kien asked.

"She would have told me if she wasn't feeling well," Ngoc said, frowning

Mai spent the sultry afternoon with Kien, trying to practice writing the English alphabet, her eyes popping up from the paper every minute to survey the beach. Then the foursome squatted around the fire pit for the evening meal, eating slowly in a depressed silence.

"When was the last time you saw her, Ngoc?" Kien asked.

Ngoc finished swallowing her mouthful of rice. "She

was in the tent with me. She told me she was going out to look at the stars. I fell asleep before she came back. I never thought…" Ngoc began to cry. "I should have stayed awake until she came back. I should have gone with her."

"Something might have happened to her on the beach last night," Mai said. "Does it look like she slept in her hammock?"

"No. Her blanket was folded," Ngoc said.

"Were there any soldiers around here last evening?" asked Mai, remembering the Malaysian soldier she and Lan had seen coming out of the woods.

"No soldiers," Kien said.

"We've got to find her." Mai's voice was insistent. "Before it's too late."

The three stared at Mai.

"You don't think she'd harm herself, do you?" Kim asked.

Mai's eyes gave the answer. *Dying of love might not just be in operas, she thought.*

"Maybe she has gone to the mainland to make sure Hiep's body has been properly buried," Kien said.

Mai brightened. "Let's go to the pier and see if anyone has seen her leaving the island."

"I'll go with you, Mai. Kim and Ngoc, why don't you stay here in case she returns?" Kien brushed the strands of dark hair from his eyes. Mai loved those eyes, blue as the sky. They made her feel safe. If anything happened to Kien, she would not know what to do. Would she run away? Would she die of sadness? Kien held her hand as they walked down the beach to the rock crossing. His hand, so solid, so strong.

She tightened her grip. Kien turned and looked at her. He squeezed her hand and continued walking.

No one had seen Lan at the Red Cross tent. No one had seen Lan at the pier. No one had seen Lan at the market. They questioned children playing in the waves, women carrying water from the wells, men unloading cabbages by the food tent. They called Lan's name from the edge of the jungle to the ocean's waves, but there was no answer.

Where was she? How could she disappear on such a small island? Mai thought of the jungle, the dense undergrowth, the mountains, their steep cliffs. A place where no one ventured.

Discouraged, Mai and Kien picked up their canned food and returned to the camp.

"Maybe Lan has come back while we were gone," Mai said, hoping that they had all been worried for nothing.

"Wouldn't that be great?" Kien answered, his voice hoarse from calling Lan's name.

But Lan hadn't returned and Mai wasn't sure what else to do. Didn't she know they were sad enough without having to worry about her? How selfish of her. She would tell Lan how angry she was when she returned. She watched the young men and women carrying water, washing dishes, building fires as if nothing had happened. Mai listened for Lan's lilting voice above the singsong chatter, imagining her running down the beach laughing at them for worrying about her. Why had Lan disappeared?

When the darkness draped the island with a sequined stretch of velvet, Mai shivered even though the night air was warm. Lan was still gone. Kien, Kim, and Ngoc huddled together by the fire. Kien was the first to speak.

"Should we ask the soldiers? Maybe they've seen her. They're supposed to be protecting us."

"No. We can't trust them. If she tried to sneak away from the island, they'll just punish her." Mai's arm brushed against his.

"It's so hard to wait," Ngoc complained.

"Where might she have gone?" asked Kien. He looked at Kim, who sat silently regarding them. "What do you think, Kim? You haven't spoken."

"My heart is too sad," whispered Kim, wringing her hands.

"I'm still thinking about that cry I heard last night. What if it was Lan? What if someone attacked her?" Mai clenched her hands. "We should search the beach."

"But you're the only one who heard it. No one else did," said Ngoc.

"Maybe you were sleeping too soundly. I might have been dreaming, but maybe not. It's worth a look." Mai looked at Kien.

"I'll go with you. We might find something," Kien replied.

After a dinner of rice and sea cucumber prepared by Ngoc, Mai and Kien walked in the wet sand, watching the waves curl and crash while the horizon swallowed the egg-round sun.

"What's that?" Mai asked. A wave had deposited a single dép on the beach. Kien walked over the picked it up, dangling it between his fingers.

"Look, there's another one." Mai pointed to a spot farther down the beach. She ran to pick it up before the waves came and reclaimed it. "They match," she said holding the lone black dép next to the one Kien held. "And they're both the same size."

She held them sole to sole. Small, a woman's. It wasn't the first time she'd discovered objects on the beach. Fishing boats packed with refugees had been landing almost weekly. She knew that many didn't make it. Tales of broken engines and men, women, and children adrift in the ocean with nothing to eat for days haunted her. Thai pirates often attacked, throwing refugees overboard to be eaten by sharks, remnants of their meager belongings washing upon the island's shore.

Mai carried the dép back to their tent, followed by Kien. Was Kien thinking what she was thinking? *I have to show these to Ngoc, just to make sure*, she thought. Strange, she had spent so much time with Lan, but she couldn't remember what her dép looked like. Ngoc would know.

Mai handed them to Ngoc. Ngoc held one in each hand and gingerly turned them over. She traced her finger around the edge of one, feeling the wetness of the rubber. A tear rolled down her cheek and dropped onto the sole of the dép. She handed them back to Mai and nodded. "Where did you find them?" she asked.

"By the water's edge. Down there." Mai pointed toward the spot.

"They look like hers. The left one had a hole in the bottom." Ngoc ran the tip of her finger around a small hole in the rubber sole.

"Maybe she went for a swim and forgot them," Kien said, his arms folded across his chest.

"She doesn't know how to swim." Ngoc knelt and placed the dép carefully on the sand, next to each other.

Abandoned. Lost. Mai's chest hurt looking at them.

"I'm tired. I need to lie down," Ngoc whispered, slipping inside the tent.

"I'm going to go with her," Mai said to Kien. "She shouldn't be alone."

She found Ngoc curled into a tight round ball on her sleeping mat, her eyes fixed on the tarp above her. "Ngoc, we'll find her. She couldn't have gone very far."

Ngoc turned her head toward Mai, her eyes red and swollen from weeping. "It's all my fault," she cried.

"What is it, Ngoc? What are you talking about?" A prickling sensation ran up Mai's arms as she leaned over.

Ngoc croaked, "There's something I haven't told you. I haven't told anyone. It's a secret."

"Is it about Lan? Tell me." Mai grabbed Ngoc's arm and pulled it toward her. Ngoc yelped. Mai released her grip and saw her fingerprints on Ngoc's flesh. Ngoc looked at her and then at her arm.

"You mustn't tell. Our family honor would be ruined." Ngoc's voice was so quiet Mai had to move close, so close she could feel the soft wind of Ngoc's breath on her cheek. "Before Hiep died…"

"Yes?" Mai's neck began to hurt.

"Before Hiep died she told me why she was no longer able to eat in the morning." Ngoc interlaced her fingers as if she were holding the secret inside them.

Mai had no idea what Ngoc was talking about. Was Lan

sick? If she was sick, she would have gone to the clinic, not run away.

"She stopped her *kinh*, her monthly bleeding." Ngoc gave Mai a knowing look, but Mai still didn't understand what Ngoc was saying. She had heard the girls talking, saying their *kinh* didn't come some months because of lack of food. But there was another reason to skip your *kinh*... An ominous reason. Mai bit the inside of her lip.

"She's going to have a baby," Ngoc gulped, her cheeks blushing pink as the sky at sunset. She averted her eyes from Mai's.

"No, that can't be," said Mai. "You must be mistaken. Who? How?"

Then she remembered Small Auntie's words when she'd explained the blood between Mai's legs. *Some day you will have babies.* But didn't you have to be married to have babies?

"Lan wasn't married. How could she have a baby?" Mai asked.

Ngoc frowned at her. "You don't have to be married to have a baby."

"Not Lan, not Lan. She's not a bad girl," Mai cried, sinking to her knees, her hands tearing at her blouse. Ngoc stroked Mai's hair.

"No, Mai, she's not a bad girl. She just made a mistake, but it's a mistake that could ruin her honor and our family's. She was very upset. I'm afraid of what she might do."

Mai turned her head and pulled Ngoc's face to hers. "Who is the father? Who would have done this terrible thing?" she demanded.

"She told me," breathed Ngoc. "It was Hiep."

Mai dropped her hands and dug her nails into her bare legs. "But I thought … I thought …"

"I know. They were very careful to keep their love a secret. But Lan couldn't keep it a secret from me. She had to tell someone she was going to have a baby. She doesn't want to have the baby without Hiep."

"We have to find her," said Mai, tugging at Ngoc's wrist. "We can't let her do anything to herself or the baby. Uncle Hiep's baby."

How happy they could all have been, with Lan and Hiep married and a baby to take care of. A little miracle out of all this sadness. A baby to hold and love and remind them that despite all the killing, there was still some beauty in life, some innocence. If they found Lan, Mai could help her with the baby, and they could make up a story about it. The baby's parents had died and they had offered to care for it, raise it. Mai knew many refugee families who had taken in orphaned children. That was it: the baby was an orphan. It wouldn't be easy. The doctor, maybe he would help. When she told Ngoc her plan, Ngoc just stared at her, unblinking.

"I need to talk to the doctor. Maybe Lan told him her secret. Maybe he can help us."

"But I asked you not to tell anyone. Please, Mai. Our family's honor …"

Mai remembered her father reminding her to always uphold their family's honor. Sometimes that's all you had left. "Maybe I could just ask the American doctor if he has *seen* Lan. That wouldn't give away her secret."

"All right," Ngoc conceded, "but please don't tell him she's pregnant."

"You're right. I won't go. I don't think he would know anything. She would have been too ashamed to go to him. But where could she be?" Mai wondered.

Just then Kim and Kien returned from gathering firewood, their arms laden with twigs from the jungle. Mai turned away from them and went into her tent. She didn't want them to see her now. She needed to sit by herself and pray for Lan, for the baby. She would have been happy to have Lan in their family. She pictured Lan and Hiep in their beautiful clothes on their wedding day, Hiep in a handsome dark suit, Lan in a red *áo dai*, her face radiant with happiness, marrying for love.

If only, if only ... there were too many "if onlys" on this island. If only Small Auntie's husband had not died in the well cave-in, Hiep might be alive. If only Mai had held onto the gold bracelet, their luck would not have run out. If only Lan had told them she was pregnant, they could have helped her. If only, if only she could tell Kien about Lan. But she had to keep the secret for Lan's sake.

Mai wondered about getting pregnant. She knew it had something to do with touching a boy, and she had been frightened the first time Kien tried to hold her hand. She had pulled away, embarrassed, and he had looked hurt. When she'd told Kim about it, Kim laughed and assured her that was not how babies were made. Kim had not elaborated, and Mai had not asked her although she was very curious. It had something to do with that blood between her legs. How she hated that monthly stream. Especially having to wear that rag, hot and bothersome, and smelly.

"Mai, are you all right?" Kien stood on the other side of the rice bag partition. Mai wiped her eyes with the edge of her blouse and pinched her cheeks.

"What do you want?" she asked.

"I have some news about Lan." Kien's voice was solemn.

"Come in. What is it?" Mai sat up on the bench, her legs folded beneath her.

"Some fishermen … early this morning … "

"Tell me. You have to tell me." Mai scrambled off the bench and stood facing Kien.

"They found a young girl's body floating in the water." Kien raked his hand through his hair.

"Is it Lan? Where is she?"

"The body is at the clinic. No one has identified it yet. I just heard from some women who were getting food. We should go see if it's her."

"Does Ngoc know?" Mai could feel the soft ocean breeze as it blew through the tent and tossed the hanging rice bags aside.

"Yes, Kim is telling her now. It might not be Lan. Many bodies are found out there when fishing boats hit the coral reefs and break up."

Mai remembered the bodies lying in the sand behind the clinic. Mothers and fathers with children, who had braved the ocean to escape to freedom. Not the freedom the Communists offered, of re-education camps and killing, but the freedom they'd had before the Americans left and the Communists had taken over South Vietnam. Only to die in the sea. But Lan was brave. Lan was strong. And Lan was lucky. *Oh, Lan, you have traveled so far. Please, please, don't let this be you.*

The four friends trudged in the twilight down the beach to the clinic, crossing at the rocks with ease because of the low water level. The blood-red sun hovered on the horizon, slowly dying to the night while the waves moaned beneath it. Mai dragged her feet in the sand, her depleted body no longer a part of her, merely a puppet that she manipulated.

She remembered the pregnant woman who had died on the fishing boat. She remembered her husband's wails and how she had covered her ears. She remembered the splash as the body slipped into the sea. *Please Buddha, please. Don't let it be her.* Did she want it to be someone else? Yes, she did.

She remembered the first time she'd met Lan. The mole on her cheek, the way her hair fell over her eyes. The gentle touch of her hand as she proclaimed them family. The offer of her mother's ring. She'd been more of a sister than her own sister.

Lan had helped her survive life on the island, where the days dragged by with a dreary sameness she had not anticipated, a dreamlike existence of work-filled mornings drawing water and standing in line for food and hotter-than-she-could-bear afternoons spent languishing in her hammock, even the flies too hot to circle above her.

Hiep, the playboy. She had heard these words in laughing asides from her cousins, their hands cupped to their mouths, but without understanding what they meant. Hiep had had a gentle, easy manner that the girls had always liked. If Lan was dead, it was his fault. His fault. No one else's. Maybe that was why he had died. Guilty of two deaths, Lan's and Sang's. *Oh, Uncle Hiep, you're not who I thought you were.*

Her lungs expanded, gasping for air, thinking of Lan walking into the sea, swallowing the salt water, the sea swallowing her and her unborn baby. Conscious of each breath she took, Mai wondered what it felt like to struggle for air as the salt water seeped into your lungs until you could do nothing but surrender

Shadows danced on tent walls illuminated by homemade candles. A baby's hungry whimper, the clucking sound of a mother's voice somewhere in the night: *no, no, not now.* Behind the Red Cross tent, a young man lifted the blanket off the figure prone in the sand. He knelt next to her holding a candle near her face, rotating it so that the dark did not mask her features, and through the wavering light Mai could see the dried salt crystals flecking the black hair matted against the hollow cheeks, the thin line of her nose, the arch of her brow and the lips, dark and swollen. And the mole. Where was the mole? She needed the mole.

"Move the candle." Mai knelt next to the body, brushed the matted hair aside, and touched the waxen cheek. Smooth and unmarked as a perfect pearl. The candle wick sputtered and the light dimmed.

"No mole," she said the words out loud to Ngoc, Kim, and Kien, who were circled around the corpse. "No mole." Leaning over the body, she pointed with her index finger at the unmarked cheek. Then she stood up and smiled slightly at the others, digging her hands into her pockets.

"We have another body over here," said the young man, pointing to a shape in the shadows. "She was found along the shore this morning. Do you want to look?" He held the candle suspended above the second corpse.

Mai peered down at a gray-haired woman, her face a forest of wrinkles. She shook her head and walked back to the first corpse.

"We've got to bury them in the morning. The heat," the young man added apologetically, covering the dead girl's face with the blanket as if he were tucking in a child at bedtime.

"But what if someone is looking for her?" Mai edged away from the dead girl. Whose daughter was she? Was there someone out there missing her? Or had they all drowned?

"We get so many bodies. They have to be buried." The young man shrugged his shoulders. Not his decision. Not his responsibility, thought Mai. What if it were his sister, dead and unidentified?

"We do keep photos so that relatives can identify them. But there are so many. So many no one knows. The boats sink and the ocean casts them on our shore. Some dead. Some alive. Luck. You've got to be lucky." He wiped his hands on his shorts and cleared his throat. "You could always put your sister's name on the Red Cross bulletin board as a missing person."

Mai eyed Ngoc, who stared at the ground, her hands clasped.

"That's a good idea," Kien said.

"No," Ngoc said, her jaw tense. "No. We'll find her." The wick on the candle had burned down to the oil, shrinking the flame to a pinpoint. "Thank you for your help," Ngoc said to the young man, backing away from the bodies.

Mai reached for her hand and Ngoc let her take it. The four followed the ocean's edge, the roar of the waves crescendoing against the darkness.

If you wanted to run away on an island, where would you go? You couldn't go far. But you could hide if someone helped you. The pregnancy would become a problem once Lan started to show. How would she explain it? She would be an outcast. Mai's head throbbed.

"She could have gone to the mainland," Kim said.

"Impossible," countered Ngoc. "You can't just get on a boat. You have to have permission."

Mai shook her head. She was certain Lan was dead. The image of the drowned girl wouldn't leave her. In her mind, she could see Lan's face on the body.

Kien brushed some sand off his leg and looked at Mai. "We'll find her." He touched her chin. She stared into his eyes. "Let's sleep. Tomorrow we can start again."

They slept on the beach that night, under a palm tree curled up in a circle, too tired to go back to camp, and it was too late anyway. The mournful pounding of the waves was their lullaby. Mai dreamed of Lan's ghost gliding along the beach, holding a baby in her arms. The baby made no sound and did not move.

Hunger pangs woke her. The sun sat on the horizon, staring at her. She woke the others and they stood in line for their breakfast rations, cream-filled rolls and canned goods.

"I think I'll stay down here and look around," Ngoc said, licking her fingers after stuffing the roll in her mouth.

"Me too," Mai offered, her stomach satisfied.

Kim and Kien wanted to stay too, but Ngoc shook her head. "Go back to camp. Maybe Lan has returned. We'll be there in a little while."

Kim hesitated, but Ngoc turned and walked away from her. Kim picked up the bag of canned food she had collected and frowned. Kien reached for Mai's bag of food.

"Here, let me carry this back for you. It's heavy, and it will be easier to search for Lan if you don't have to carry this."

Mai handed him the bag, their fingers touching and lingering together for a moment. How she wanted to tell him. She hated keeping a secret from him.

"Thanks," she whispered.

Kien ambled down the beach with Kim, swinging the bags as he took long strides to Kim's short mincing steps.

A throng of people crowded the pier, bags in their hands, waiting to board a small ship. Mai could hear their excited chatter. A woman with four children—one in her arms, another clinging to her blouse, and two holding hands behind her—stood in the back of the line. Mai could see the woman's profile as she turned her head. Small Auntie.

Mai inhaled. They were leaving. This was the day. She wished she could say goodbye to the children. What would Small Auntie say if she went over to them? Did she know Minh had given her the bracelet? It was too late for her to try to take the bracelet away again. Mai wanted to say goodbye. She might never see them again.

"Wait for me here. I have something to do," she said to Ngoc. She moved across the beach, where she could hear a man in uniform with a clipboard calling out names. The line started to move. Mai worked her short legs faster, faster. The passengers were boarding. She stepped out of her dép and barreled through the sand in her bare feet. "Minh, Minh, wait!"

Minh turned his head, but Small Auntie jerked him ahead of her onto the boat. Mai ran up on the pier as the captain gunned the engine. She could see Minh staring at her, his dark eyes searching under a shock of dark, shaggy hair. She waved, but he just stared at her.

As the boat turned to head out to the mainland, she saw a familiar figure crouched in the bow. She squinted in the sun. Their eyes met, and Mai waved and called to her. The girl's hand moved in reply, as if in slow motion, and then she disappeared from sight. It was Lan.

Eighteen

Mai remained on the pier, her bare feet planted on its bamboo planks, arms waving, eyes squinting into the hazy blue of the sky. She watched the boat turn into a black speck on the far horizon, listened to the whine of its engine mingling with the cadence of the waves. Rubbing her eyes, she strained to track it, but the sun's rays danced on the ocean's surface, blinding her.

"Mai, Mai, Mai," echoed from the beach, but she stood like a stone, face toward the sea, feeling the waves hitting the pier, the rise and fall of her chest, her throat aching, the sun rippling across the boards beneath her. She squeezed her eyes together harder and pictured Lan peering over the railing. Had her lips moved? Had she tried to tell her something? *Why are you on the boat, Lan? Where are you going?*

A gull winged overhead, its screech bouncing off her eardrums. She crumpled against a post and stared at the bird circling above her. Oh, to be free like that, free to go anywhere, free to fly away from this island, this prison. Lan had flown away. She could too. She would fly away to freedom. She wanted to leap off the pier and flap her arms into the air.

When she was four, her brother Loc had dared her to jump from the mango tree in the orchard. *Like the birds. Easy. Flap your arms. Faster. Faster. Now. Jump. Down, down, down.* Her small body had piled in a heap. When Ba Du had called out, she ran to her, scolding her brother. No broken bones. A headache for two days. No, she would not do anything so foolish again, she had promised her worried parents.

"Mai, what's the matter? You look as if you've seen a ghost?" Kien scuttled up the ramp and peered down at her.

She grabbed his outstretched hand. She wanted to tell him what she had seen, but her mind began to play tricks on her. Had it really been Lan? Perhaps it had been a ghost. *Ghosts.* Goose bumps grew on her arms, even though the sun's rays had begun to fry the day.

"Kien." Mai searched his eyes, hoping he would believe her. "I saw Lan on the boat. She's going to the mainland."

"Are you sure it was her? How could she have gotten on? They check everyone's papers." Kien shoved his hands deep into his pockets, scowling.

"I saw her, and she saw me. She called out, but I couldn't hear her." Mai's voice rose in indignation at not being believed. Retreating from the pier, she picked up her dép from the sand, shook them off, and balanced first on one foot and then the other to slip them on. Kien reached out to help her but she pushed his arm away.

"Don't be angry, Mai. It's just that it's so hard to believe. Why would Lan want to run away?"

Kien put his arm around her, and this time she did not reject him. How could she tell him Lan's secret? She had promised Ngoc that she wouldn't tell anyone. No, not even Kien.

"I don't know," she lied, "but we have to tell Ngoc. She will be so relieved that Lan is alive."

Nausea gripped her as she spoke. She loved Kien. How could she lie to him? Maybe it wasn't really a lie. Breaking your promise was worse. Father had said never to lie and never to break a promise. She didn't know what to do. But they had to go tell Ngoc. Maybe she would tell Kien why Lan had run away. *If* she had run away.

Ngoc sobbed when Mai told her that she had seen Lan on the boat. "She's alive. Thank you, thank you," she said.

Neither Mai nor Ngoc gave any indication that they knew that Lan was pregnant. Later, when they were alone, Ngoc spoke to her.

"I hope you haven't told anyone what I told you about Lan. She must have had an important reason to leave the island without me." Ngoc brushed her cheek with her hand and stared at Mai.

"No," Mai replied. "But you know, it might not have been Lan. Someone looking like her, maybe."

"I must find out. Maybe the doctor knows something." Ngoc traced her foot in the sand. "He could be counted on to keep her secret." She sought Mai's face for confirmation. Mai looked away.

The doctor was busy with a patient when Mai and Ngoc arrived at the clinic, so they sat in the sand near the entrance to the tent and waited, their legs crossed, their eyes fixed on the tent opening. Mai imagined Lan on the Malaysian mainland, her stomach bulging with the new life within her, giving birth, taking care of a baby by herself, hungry and alone, crying in grief for Hiep.

"The doctor can see you now," the nurse said, waving them into the tent.

The doctor smiled. It was the same doctor who had treated Hiep.

"What can I do for you?" he said, running his hands through his thinning hair.

"It's about my sister, Lan." Ngoc turned her head to see if the nurse was listening. Relieved that they were alone, she continued. "She's missing, and we're worried. We thought you might know something."

The doctor scratched his ear.

What does he know? thought Mai.

"We had to send her to the mainland to the hospital today," he finally said.

"Why? What's the matter with her?" Ngoc pleaded, looking up at him.

Mai bit her lower lip.

"The matter is rather private. Is it all right if I speak in front of her?" he asked, nodding toward Mai.

"Oh, yes, she's like a sister," Ngoc said, pulling Mai close to her.

"Lan came in early this morning, bleeding and in a great deal of pain." He stopped and drove his hands deep into the pockets of his white coat.

"Why was she bleeding?" Ngoc asked.

"Do you know she is pregnant?" he replied.

Ngoc nodded slowly and held her breath.

"The baby? Is the baby all right?" Mai asked. Perhaps it really was Lan who had cried out in the night.

"I hope so. We stopped the bleeding, but I sent her to the mainland to have a specialist examine her in the hospital. She wanted to tell you she was leaving, but there was no time. Would you like to go see her?"

"Oh, yes," cried Ngoc and Mai in chorus.

The doctor shook his head. "I'm sorry, but only a relative can visit." He looked at Ngoc. "You'll have to go by yourself. She may need you to stay a while."

Mai turned to Ngoc. "Don't worry. I'll tell the others Lan is sick. We don't need to say anything else."

Tears welled in Ngoc's eyes. "I'm so grateful to you. I'll send you a letter as soon as I can." Turning to the doctor, she asked, "How soon can I leave?"

"I'll be going back to the mainland after lunch. You can come with me then."

"Oh, thank you, thank you," Ngoc said, bowing from the waist, clenching her hands. "I'll go get my things."

"Meet me back here after lunch and we'll go together. Now, if you'll excuse me, I have more patients to attend to." He turned to go.

Mai felt a twinge of envy as she and Ngoc padded along the beach. She knew she shouldn't feel this way. How could she be envious of Ngoc going to see Lan in the hospital? But she was. She had been on this island for almost a year. What was the mainland like? What was happening in the rest of the world?

"What are you thinking?" Ngoc asked, reaching for Mai's hand.

Mai turned her face away from Ngoc and didn't answer. How could she mask her jealousy? Would Ngoc and Lan leave her here? Would she ever see them again?

"I was just thinking about Lan. I wish I could go with you."

"I wish you could come. I'm afraid to go by myself, but I know Lan needs me." Ngoc stepped over a rock in the sand. "I'm so worried about the baby."

The baby. Hiep's baby. *Oh*, Mai prayed, *please don't let Lan lose this baby.* It would be like Hiep dying a second time. Mai did not know what this kind of bleeding meant, but she knew it was a bad omen. Was it like the monthly bleeding? Why would you bleed when you were pregnant? She wished she could have asked the doctor, but she was too shy. Maybe Ngoc knew. No, she couldn't ask Ngoc. It would just make her worry more.

After lunch, Ngoc came to Mai's tent, her hands shaking, her black eyes somber. "I'm going now. You can tell the others Lan is sick after I leave. I didn't want to tell anyone. Too many questions. I know you can handle it."

Mai cleared her throat. "I'll be waiting. I'll pray for Lan's good health. Want me to walk to the boat with you?"

Ngoc pushed back her shoulders. "No need. You stay here. I'll be seeing you soon."

Mai sank onto her bed after Ngoc left, a feeling of helplessness cascading over her. Hiep was gone, and now Lan and Ngoc. She picked up her knitting and thought of making something for the baby. Or would that bring bad luck? She dropped her needles in her lap and stared out at the ocean. A whole world out there and she was trapped on this speck of earth. If she ever got off this island, she never wanted to see the ocean again.

Later that afternoon, Kien poked his head through the tent flap to ask if she had found out anything more about Lan. Mai told him that Lan had gone to the hospital on the mainland, and then she looked away.

Kien wasn't fooled. "There's something you're not telling me, isn't there?"

Mai shook her head. "No, Kien, I'm just worried about her. When Uncle Hiep went to the hospital, he didn't come back," she said, her words ending in a sob.

Kien reached for Mai's hand. She felt the warmth of his skin as their fingers intertwined."How stupid of me. Of course, you're worried. I'm sorry. I was just so happy that we had found Lan."

"I know, I know." Mai sighed, hoping Kien's questions had ended, as she stared into his eyes. Kien moved closer to her and drew her to him, his arms holding her close. She started to withdraw but stopped, melting into him, feeling the warmth of his body against hers. She trembled as he cupped his hands around her chin and leaned over, his lips touching hers, first gently, like the kiss of a butterfly, and then more firmly, his eyes wide open looking into hers.

She pushed him away. "Don't do that."

Kien stepped back, dropped his hands to his sides, and then turned and left the tent, shoulders stiff and head held high. Mai watched him disappear through the opening. His lips had been rough, chapped by the sun, but oh, so sweet. His breath was warm and soft on her cheek; his hands rough but gentle. A shiver shot from Mai's neck to her toes. She touched her cheek. Traced her finger over her lips. Is this what Lan and Hiep had felt? Look what had happened to them.

Her mother's voice spoke inside her head, warning her: *Stay away from boys, keep yourself pure.* But Mai had not really understood what she meant. Now she knew how delicious it felt to have a boy hold you, kiss you. It wasn't going to be easy.

She darted to the tent opening and peered out. Where was he? What was she going to do? She spotted him down near the water, sitting cross-legged in the sand and throwing pebbles into the waves. She wanted to go to him, but she was afraid. Afraid of what she might say. Afraid that what had happened to Lan might happen to her. Could you get pregnant by kissing? She didn't think so. It was what happened after the kissing. She could feel her cheeks turning red with shame. She hunched down and hugged her knees tight to her chest, resting her cheek on them and longing to kiss him again. Was she a bad girl? She didn't know. She was all mixed up.

That night she lay in her hammock a long time watching Hiep's empty hammock sway in the breeze, worrying about Lan, listening to the crashing chorus of the ocean, and missing her family and the quiet of her home near the rice paddies. She was all alone, and she was sure that Kien would never speak to her again. She had looked for him that evening but was relieved she hadn't found him

When she awoke, she stepped onto the sandy ground

and pushed the hanging rice bag aside to peer out. A shaft of sun grazed her cheek. Well, at least she wouldn't have to walk through the rain to get the morning's rations. As she reached up to retrieve the string bag on the hook above Hiep's hammock, a dozen conversations went through her head. Kien would probably be in line at the food tent. *"I'm sorry. You surprised me."* No, that wouldn't do. *"Why did you do that?"* No, that was stupid and would only embarrass him.

Would she have the courage to tell him she liked it, that she felt the same way about him? No, that might really get her in trouble. Maybe he would speak first. Or ignore her. Bile inched its way up her throat and she knelt, gagging and retching, the thick liquid pouring out of her mouth onto the sand, its stench invading her nostrils, making her retch again.

She kicked some sand over the vomit and wiped her lips, recoiling from the bitter taste. The string bag lay on the ground where she had dropped it. Picking it up, she headed toward the food distribution center though she had no desire to eat. She just wanted to see him.

She joined the line behind a slender young woman with a child nestled against her, her arm supporting his bottom. Small dark eyes opened wide over his mother's shoulder. A tiny hand reached out to touch her. Mai moved closer and caught his finger in hers. He laughed and tried to pull it away. Mai let go and smiled at him. How she missed her family. The line moved, and she continued to wait.

"Don't just stand there. Where's your ticket?" a voice barked at her, breaking her reverie. Mai pulled a small slip of paper from her pocket. She held out her bag as the breakfast rolls and canned goods were dropped in.

Above the morning hum of the crowd, the loudspeaker blasted a string of names. She cocked her head. Dropped her bag and froze. Her name. "Nguyen Mai" in the air. Floating toward her. Freedom. A sob.

No one glanced her way. There were names every day, but only yours counted. She picked up her bag and ran to find Kien. But you didn't always leave right away. She knew that. She had to have a physical, and then she would have to wait again. The ship would be next.

No Kien. She danced back to their camp, calling for him. His name bounced off the rocks, echoed off the waves, settled in the sand. She glanced around the inside of the tent that she and Hiep had shared. What would she take? The red cloth bag she had carried from Vietnam, a couple of pieces of clothing, the bracelet. She glanced at the fire pit. She would dig it out after her physical. No time now. And someone might see. Kien—she had to talk to Kien.

There was a shadow at the entrance to her tent. Like a statue in the doorway, not moving. She hoped it was Kien.

"Kien, did you hear? My name … I'm leaving."

He cracked his knuckles.

"Are you angry with me? Don't be angry. You can't be. I'm leaving."

"I heard. I heard." His shoulders slumped.

"I'm sorry about yesterday." She stumbled toward him and placed her hands in his. "It's all my fault. No one has ever kissed me before. Not like that."

His frown was replaced by the slip of a smile that settled on the corners of his mouth. He shifted his weight from one foot to the other.

Then he spoke. "I'll miss you."

"I'll miss you too."

So he didn't want to talk about the kiss. Mai felt relief. Pain. Pain in her chest. Hard to breathe. Missing him already. "We may never see each other again," she whispered, squeezing his hands tighter, her chest pounding with pain.

"My name will be called soon, I'm sure. Maybe I'll go to America too." Kien cleared his throat and dropped her hands.

"Oh, I hope so. I was just looking at my things." Mai swept her arm around the tent. "There's not much. Would you like some dishes and pans? Something to remember me by." She laughed.

"I'll remember you. I don't need anything," Kien replied. She smiled at him through her tears. He reached over and wiped them away with his thumbs.

"I'll remember you too," she said, feeling the warmth of his skin on hers. Would she ever see him again? The excitement of leaving. The sorrow of leaving.

"When will you leave?" Kien asked, his face solemn.

"I don't know. I have to go to the clinic first. After lunch. They don't let you go if you're sick. Oh, you don't think they'll stop me, do you?" Her knees buckled and Kien caught her before she fell.

"What's the matter?" he said, his arms steadying her.

Mai coughed and tried to stand.

"Have you eaten today?"

She shook her head. She'd been too excited to eat. The bag of food was on the floor. Kien reached into it and grabbed a roll. Breaking off a bite, he held it to her lips. She could smell its sweet aroma. She took it from his hand and devoured it.

"You have to come with me," she said, wiping the crumbs off her lips.

"I can't. Not until my name is called."

"No, to the clinic. I'm afraid."

"I'll come. Now eat the rest of the roll. I'll get you some water."

Revived, Mai perched on the bench and ate another roll. She could hear the clink of the tin cup as Kien banged it against the edge of the water bucket. She took the cup from his hand, their fingers touching. The warm water slid down her throat. Kien sat next to her, so close his breath was a warm breeze on her neck. She could feel their knees touching.

"Kien, if I tell you something, will you promise never to tell anyone?"

Kien peered down at her. She knew she had promised Ngoc not to tell, but Ngoc would need someone to help her and Lan. Kien would have to know. The secret was too heavy for Ngoc to carry by herself.

"What is it?"

"Promise. You must promise."

"Of course."

She stared at her feet, not daring to look him in the eye. She had promised Ngoc. Would breaking a promise bring bad luck? Maybe not, if the promise were broken for a good reason.

"Kien, remember when I told you I thought I saw Lan on the boat?"

"Yes." He turned his face toward her and tried to catch her eyes, but she kept her head down.

"It was her. I found out why she left," Mai whispered.

Kien was silent, waiting.

"She's going to have a baby. Ngoc told me. She's gone to the hospital on the mainland. Ngoc went to be with her."

The words rushed out in a torrent, as if she was afraid they wouldn't come out at all unless she pushed them out all at once. Now what had she done? Kien would want nothing to do with such a bad girl. If he found out that Hiep was the father, he would want nothing to do with Mai either. Her family honor had been ruined.

She held her breath, waiting for his reaction. She would not have been surprised if he had risen and left her, but he didn't. Instead, he pushed back his shoulders and sat up straight.

"What can I do to help?" he said, biting his lower lip.

"I just needed to share this with you. Lan and Ngoc might need your help after I'm gone. I'm so worried."

She wanted to tell him that Hiep was the father, but she felt she had told too much.

"Who is the father?" Kien asked, reading her mind. "He should be the one helping her." His voice grew gruff.

"He can't. He's dead."

"Dead? But who?" Kien stopped. "Hiep. Is it Hiep?"

Mai just nodded, her chin quivering. Now Kien would want nothing to do with any of them. "I won't blame you if you want nothing to do with us. Both our families have been dishonored."

He sat down and cracked his knuckles.

"I'm sorry I told you. I just had to." Mai ran her fingers through her tangled hair. "Are you shocked?"

Finally Kien spoke. "What do you want me to do?"

Mai's lips parted into a thin smile. "Thank you. I was afraid you would think…"

Kien shook his head, interrupting her. "Have you forgotten? My parents weren't married. No time. War. Who knows how much time there is?"

"But Kien, what about the rules?" Mai's voice quivered.

"What rules?" he said, his eyes widening.

"The ones we grew up with," Mai whispered.

"The rules?" Kien scoffed. "Look at what has happened to our country and to us. Do you think anybody cares about the rules? I just want to survive." He pounded his fist on the bench.

Mai gaped at him, never having heard him talk like this. She thought of her parents, of the orderly life they had lived in Vietnam, where everyone knew his place, boys and girls were carefully chaperoned, and marriages were arranged. But Hiep and Lan had broken the rules, and they had been punished. Fear swallowed Mai. Fear for Lan and her baby. *Please, dear Buddha, they've been punished enough.* She could see Kien's eyes gazing at her. Would they meet again in America?

"I have to go the clinic," she said, pointing to the tent opening.

"I'll come with you."

"No, it's okay."

He followed her out of the tent and smiled, his white

teeth flashing in the sunlight. "Thank you for telling me your secret. Don't worry. I won't tell."

She gave him a brief look of thanks and turned to go.

Nineteen

Mai traipsed through the hot sand to the Red Cross clinic, her mind a muddle. She was relieved that Kien had been understanding, sad about having to leave without him, and worried about the physical. Her stomach churned. She walked straight to the clinic, and the sun bounced off her *non lá* as she squatted in line, waiting. The woman ahead of her shuffled forward, and she moved forward. Every inch brought her closer to the test, the test that would determine her fate.

Women were directed to the left, into one tent, and men to the right. Mai walked slowly, without comprehending what was happening. Once inside the tent, she saw groups of women undressing and huddling together.

"What are they going to do to us?" she asked a sallow-faced girl who was slipping off her dép.

The girl continued to undress without answering her.

"Take off all your clothes and line up. The doctor is going to check you," announced a slim blonde girl with a clipboard in her hand.

Mai hugged the tent wall. Never would she do that. She had undressed only in front of her mother and Small Auntie, and she would not undress in front of all these women and then have a man check her. There must be some mistake. She looked around. Several women, their eyes staring downward, were standing in line, with their hands covering their breasts and their crotches. Mai tried not to stare, but she had never seen a naked body before, not even her mother's.

The whoosh of cloth dropping to the floor filled the room. A baby screamed. She could not escape. She pulled off her blouse with wooden fingers, and then slipped off her pants. She was naked except for the blood-soaked rag between her legs. Why did it have to be now? She reached between her legs and removed the cloth, feeling the dampness, smelling the odor of the blood. Peeking at the room from the corners of her eyes, she was relieved to see that no one was looking at her. She hid the rag under her clothes and then stepped in line.

When it was her turn, the doctor moved closer until she could smell the tobacco on his breath. He motioned for her to open her mouth, then put a wooden stick on her tongue, gagging her. She squeezed her eyes shut, trying to blot out the humiliation of standing before him naked, but she had to open them when he put a cold instrument to her eyes and pulled back her eyelids. Her eyeballs felt as if they were going to pop out of her head. Mai wanted to scream, but she didn't. No amount of pain would stop her from leaving the island.

Nodding approvingly, the doctor had her turn around as he examined her fingers and her feet. Mai's cheeks burned as he touched her. Then the doctor put a cold metal stethoscope on her chest, pantomimed for her to breathe deeply, and listened. He said something she didn't understand and motioned for her to move on.

She ran to her pile of clothes and pulled them on. She had never seen this doctor before. He must be new. If Hiep's doctor had been there, she would have run from the tent rather than let him see her naked. When the woman with the clipboard checked her name off and told her that she had passed, she fell from the tent, blinded by the noonday sun. Tears clouded her eyes. Never had she felt so degraded, so embarressed.

Recovering her sight, she saw Kien leaning against a palm tree.

"I passed. I passed," she called. America was no longer a dream. Now she had to wait for the loudspeaker to call her name one more time, so she could go to the ship. It could be hours or days, but it would happen.

She leaned her head on Kien's shoulder, her tears staining his tan shirt. "I wish you were coming with me."

"Don't cry," he said smoothing her hair. "You're going to be all right." But the tears cascaded from her, kept at bay for so long that even his soft words could not stop them. How could she feel so happy, while still feeling so humiliated from the exam?

"You don't know what they did in there. I would have rather drowned in the ocean," she coughed between sobs.

Before Kien could reply, a voice boomed from the loudspeaker, rattling off a list of names and saying, "Report to the pier for immigration in two hours."

The afternoon boat. My name. Leaving. No time. Must

hurry. The boat. No time. Wipe away the tears. Forget the humil-
iation. Leaving. Goodbye. Kien. My things. Gold bracelet. Dig.
Hide it. Blouse hem. Good luck. Remember what Mother said.

Words were rushing through Mai's head faster than she could think. She ran to the camp, followed by Kien and Kim calling to her: "Wait, Mai. We'll help you."

The breeze caught her hair and flattened it against her cheeks. For a moment Mai imagined she was back home playing in the orchard, being chased by her cousins in a game of tag, smelling the sweet scent of apples overhead, hearing the lowing of a water buffalo as it sloshed through a nearby rice paddy. She could hear the patter of Kien and Kim's feet behind her as they tried to catch up.

When she reached her tent and smelled the familiar scent of rice and wood fire mixed with the briny smell of the sea, she caught her breath. There was not much to take. The bright red bag with her notebook and knitting needles, yarn, the lumpy scarf, two pairs of pants, two extra blouses. A broken pencil.

She eyed the cooking fire, the three rocks arranged in a triangle with the fire pit in the middle. Kien and Kim were standing outside the tent waiting for her, and they watched her kneel in the sand and dig her hands into the mound of ashes. She dug deep, dug for her bracelet, her fingertips feeling for the remnant of the rice bag that held it, protected it from the sand and sea. The ashes, damp and cool, turned Mai's fingers as black as the midnight sky. She pushed them into a heap and felt the gritty sand beneath, clawing at it, frantic now for the bracelet, grains of sand wedging beneath her fingernails and stinging the soft tips of her fingers.

Where is it? Hurry. Find it. Find it now. Can't leave without it. Something terrible might happen to her if she left without it. *Dig deeper, to the left, no, to the right.* Suddenly her fingers touched cloth, a stiff corner protruding like a flag; now they touched a hard metal circle, and she pulled the cloth from the pit and opened it. The gold bracelet, speckled with sand, gleaming in the sunlight, lay so still in her hand.

Kim called to her. "Hurry, Mai."

Chided like a child, Mai ran to the tent, slipped off her worn pants and blouse, and pulled out her special clothes, her "going to America" outfit—the red blouse her mother had stitched for her and the black pants. She stuffed her other clothes in her bag and eyed her dép, one with its broken strap held to the sole by a single bent nail. She picked up her bag, her eyes sweeping the small space that she and Hiep had shared: his hammock hanging limply next to hers, the hooks they'd hung their bags on, the tin can candle he'd made.

She could see him once again, his shadow dancing on the tent wall, the candle sending out its shaft of light as he bent over, writing letters to the brother he would never see again. She could hear him moaning as he lay retching in his hammock, feel his hand on hers as he lowered her into the hold of the ship. Mai stifled a sob and turned to go. There was no time to live in the past, only time to live in the present now and get on that boat.

"Kim, Kien, come here," she called, poking her head through the tent flap. They appeared. "I want you to have these." Mai pointed to the pots and pans, the can opener, and the water bucket. They could trade them at the market for food. "Oh, how I am going to miss you."

Kim and Kien did not speak. Finally Kim said, "We'll be seeing you in America. Now go on and don't worry about us." She motioned for Mai to leave.

They followed her like two puppies as she walked back to the main camp, their presence a knife cutting her happiness in half. At the Red Cross tent, she was given a clear plastic bag full of papers, a stern warning—"Don't lose these"—and a name tag. Then off to the pier.

"Don't forget to find out about Lan," she said to Kien. "You can write me at my uncle's." She handed him a slip of paper with her uncle's name and address on it.

"I'll write you," he promised, sliding his arms around her and drawing her to him.

How could she leave him? What if she stayed?

"I'm not going to leave without you," Mai said, raising her eyes to meet his. "It's no use. I'll wait until your name is called. Then we'll go together." She dropped both her bags in the sand, her red cloth bag and the plastic bag with her papers.

"No, Mai, you can't wait. You've got to leave the island and get away from Sang's ghost. It's not safe for you here. We'll meet again. I promise."

Mai lifted her face to Kien. No longer afraid, she kissed him. A long kiss. A sweet kiss. And he kissed her back. She clung to him until he had to pry her arms away.

"Please go. I love you. I don't want anything to happen to you," he said.

"And I love you. I will see you again. In America," she said. Then she turned to Kim, who had stepped back a few feet from them.

"I'll write you too," Kim said, forcing a smile. "And when we're all in America, we'll meet and have ice cream."

Mai clutched her two bags tighter, her fingernails cutting into her palms. "Goodbye," she said.

Kien tried to catch her hand, but she darted away and took her place in line. If she touched him again, the pain would be too much and she might not have the strength to leave.

"Nguyen Mai," a raspy voice bleated through a bullhorn. Pushing her way to the front, she held her identification card up to the man with the clipboard, who grabbed it between his sun-scorched fingers.

"Step aboard," he grunted, pushing the card toward her, his teeth yellowed by nicotine. Mai dropped it back into her bag and turned to look at the beach, her eyes searching for Kien, but he had disappeared into the send-off crowd that milled about the end of the pier.

"Move along," the man with the clipboard ordered.

The short gangplank that bridged the gap between the pier and the boat shifted as the waves beat against them. Holding both bags in one hand, Mai stepped on the narrow bridge, her stomach churning like the waves beneath her. She could smell the fumes from the diesel fuel, hear the whir of the engine, and feel the wind pushing her back towards the pier as if it were trying to prevent her from going. Or was it Sang's ghost still after her?

She teetered across the plank, hardly daring to believe she was leaving at last, afraid that someone would call her name and tell her she couldn't go after all. But no one did, and she boarded the boat and looked around. A fishing boat. It was larger than the one she had come on, but this time there would be no hiding, no patrol boats. She tilted her head toward the blue sky. It was all hers. Not just a single slice, as when she'd huddled in the hold gasping for air. She was going to America. To a new home. Sinking onto a bench, Mai arranged the bags on her lap and watched as the boat filled with refugees, one by one.

An emaciated young woman, a bony baby limp in her arms and a small boy clinging to her blouse, approached. Mai moved over so she could sit beside her. The woman sighed and nodded to the boy, who squeezed onto her lap, and shushed the baby who had begun to cry. When the boat was full, with people sitting or standing in every available space, the captain revved the engines. The sailors stowed the gang-plank and lifted the lines, and Mai listened to the left-behinds calling to them as they chugged across the open sea, their goodbyes fading to silence.

She closed her eyes, then opened them again, and the island had disappeared. Ghosts could not cross water. She was safe. The Malaysian mainland, small specks of trees and buildings, materialized in the distance—a promise of new adventures, of a beginning, of a new life. *But what kind of life?* Mai wondered. How long would it take to get to that new life?

She shivered and then laughed to herself, remembering that when they were on the road, she had always been the one to say to her father, "When will we be there? How much farther?" He would turn, his dark eyes dancing, and tease, "Until we get there." Then he would laugh, grab the steering wheel with one hand, and flick his cigarette ashes out the side window.

How she missed him. How she wished that he and mother and the whole family and Kien were sitting next to her on this bench right now, speeding toward a new life together.

She pulled her *non lá* over her eyes, securing the elastic strap beneath her chin, and stroked the gold bracelet deep in her pocket, praying for protection and good fortune for the rest of the journey.

The woman next to her, having finally quieted her baby, spoke. "Where are you going?"

Mai crossed her legs and looked up. "To America," she answered, trying to sound very grown-up.

"By yourself?" the woman inquired, emphasizing the last word.

"Yes." Mai turned her head and looked away. "By myself." Saying the words out loud made her feel so abandoned. What had she done to deserve this? Her chest felt hollow, her voice weak, but she remembered her father's words—"You must survive"—and felt a surge of strength shoot through her. No, she would not feel sorry for herself. She would not always be alone. Her uncle and aunt would meet her, and then soon the rest of her family would come.

"I'm going to Australia," the woman confided. "My brother is there waiting for us." She pulled her children closer to her. "I hear it's a very big place, with kangaroos."

"What's a kangaroo?" Mai asked.

"An animal that jumps on its hind legs and carries its

baby in a pouch on its stomach. My brother sent me a picture of one. Want to see?" The woman dug in her bag and extracted a crumpled picture that she held up for Mai to see.

Mai peered at it. A light brown animal standing on its hind legs with a baby sticking its head out of its stomach? What kind of animals did they have in America? She had never thought to ask her uncle. "Thanks. It's beautiful," she added politely.

Just then the boat started to slow down. The sound of the whining engine dimmed and the crowd became agitated. Standing up, Mai could see the mainland, boats of all sizes dotting the shore where several piers jutted into the ocean. After tying up to one of them, the passengers jammed the exit ramp, clutching children, carrying bags, calling to one another in high-pitched voices, their eyes hungry with hope.

A dingy yellow bus was parked across from the pier, a driver standing at its open door and beckoning to them. Mai followed the line that straggled across the parking lot and waited to board. When it was her turn, the driver, a dark-skinned man in a crumpled green uniform, extended his hand as she struggled up the steep steps. Inside, the smell of humanity, strong and musky, hit her nostrils. No salty sea air here. She inched down the narrow aisle, her bags close to her, searching for an empty seat. The young woman she'd met on the boat motioned to her.

"Sit here," she invited, moving her little boy onto her lap next to her baby. Mai sank into the vinyl seat and pushed her bags under the seat in front of her.

"Here," Mai said, "let me hold him. It's too hot to have two on your lap."

The boy's body was warm against hers, and he let out a cry when his mother handed him to Mai. Through the open window, Mai could see the pier, and their boat, now being loaded with boxes of supplies to take back to the island for the evening meal. The workers called to one another, their voices echoing against the crashing waves.

"Attention everyone. I am your driver. I will be taking you to the airport in Kuala Lumpur," announced the man in the crumpled green uniform. He adjusted his dust-coated cap, closed the bus doors, and grabbed the steering wheel. Mai settled into her seat, the gears on the bus grinding as the driver gunned the engine.

Too excited to sleep, she spent the next several hours transfixed by the verdant landscape rushing by her, the tiny roadside stands, the dense rubber-tree plantations, the rice paddies, the towering mountains. It was so much like Vietnam.

When the rain started pinging on the bus's metal roof, Mai remembered the way it had tapped against the red tile roof of her village home, the sweetness of knowing that the rice paddies would be flooded, and that the farmers, after their hard work tilling the soil trudging behind a water buffalo, would be able to scatter the seeds that would eventually sprout into *ma*, the tiny seedlings that would then be tied in bundles and replanted in larger paddies. Closing her eyes, she could see the bent backs of the villagers and hear the splish-splash of their feet as they plodded in the paddies, placing the seedlings in straight, even rows like the lines in her composition book.

The boy in her lap had fallen asleep. She closed her arms around him so he wouldn't slip off. His mother was staring out the window, tears running down her face. The baby breathed slowly, tiny eyes closed, fingers curled around her thumb. The woman saw that she was looking and raised her hand to wipe her face. Mai reached over and touched her hand.

"Don't be sad," Mai said. "We're leaving here. Everything's going to be better now."

"I know, I know," the woman replied. "It's just that..." The tears started to run down her face again. "My husband, the Thai pirates. What am I going to do without him?"

Mai had no answer. She drew the little boy closer, feeling the sweaty warmth of his body, the soft beating of his heart.

"Where is your family?" the woman asked, turning her head toward Mai, her eyes bright from crying.

"My parents are in Vietnam, I think." Mai replied. "Unless they've been able to escape. I don't know if they're dead or alive."

"Ah, you poor child. Who is going to take care of you?" the woman whispered.

"My uncle and aunt. They're waiting for me." Mai tried to sound brave.

If only there were some water to drink, but there was nothing. Her mouth burned with thirst.

The hum of the wheels rolling along the road sang Mai to sleep, and then the blare of the bus's horn and a shrill screech of brakes woke her. Her blouse and pants were soaked with sweat. Across the field, a silver airplane soared into the sky, and a gleaming building appeared with large letters over it in a language Mai could not understand.

"We are now arriving at Subang International Airport," the driver announced, turning left and driving down a long road lined with palms. It lead into the airport, where a throng of buses and cars jammed the narrow lanes.

After the bus had parked and the passengers had all filed off, they were separated into groups depending on their destinations. The young woman and her two children were whisked away by a uniformed airline attendant.

"Are you Miss Nguyen?" someone asked.

Mai looked up and saw the friendly eyes of a small pudgy man wearing a blue uniform. She nodded shyly, too excited to speak.

"Come with me. I'll take you to your airline. Going to the United States, I see?" He smiled, checking the paper in his hand and peering at her name tag.

Mai squeezed the handles of her bags tighter and followed the man into the building, to a ticket counter with the red letters *TWA* emblazoned on the wall behind it. The pudgy man talked to the woman behind the counter, who peered at Mai and then clacked her bright red nails across a keyboard. No other refugee was going to the United States on this flight. Only Mai. The hand with the long red nails handed a plane ticket to her.

Unable to read what it said, Mai held it tightly. This piece of paper with the tiny markings on it. Her pass to freedom.

The man led her to a seat in a boarding area; she could see the big number 5 on the wall. He sat next to her, explaining in Vietnamese that the plane would be leaving in less than an hour for America, stopping along the way to refuel in Narita Airport in Japan, and then on to San Francisco, USA. Strange sounding names. A woman's voice echoed over a microphone.

"Time to go," the man said. Mai hopped up after him, her stomach feeling as if it were a basket of butterflies. He led her out the door, past the airline agent, who reached for her ticket, and across the tarmac to a huge silver plane. It gleamed in the sunlight, the three gigantic red letters on the tail: *TWA*.

"Goodbye," the man said, bowing to her.

Bewildered, Mai reached for the handrail on the stairs. Shaking, she climbed the steps to the plane's entrance, where there was a stewardess in a dark blue suit and matching high heels, her hair pulled back from her carefully made-up face. Her prominent blue eyes made contact with Mai's eyes, welcoming her. Businessmen in dark suits and ties were settling into the rows of seats before her. The stewardess, seeing Mai's confusion, pointed her to a seat by the window. She slid into it, holding her bags tightly in her lap, and peered out. Below her, a long silver wing reached out from the side of the plane. On the runway, she could see a man driving a cart filled with bags alongside the plane, and in the distance, another plane rolling down the runway. Then, as if it had invisible strings on it that pulled it upward, that plane's nose went up, then its body, and finally its tail, until it was sailing through the air.

Mai's hand went to her throat and her nose pressed against the glass of the small window. Her other hand touched the buckle of the seat belt underneath her. She reached for the other end of it and buckled it around her. A young businessman in a double-breasted gray suit plopped down next to her. The sweet scent of aftershave accompanied him. In the aisle, the flight attendant was holding up a sign and making an announcement in English.

Mai waited, sitting upright in her seat, afraid to relax, as the doors closed and the airplane started to move away from the gate. She gripped the arm of her seat and held her breath, watching the ground disappear as the plane went up. There was a loud grinding sound. Then it was gone. The plane cut through the billowing clouds and climbed higher and higher while Mai clutched her mother's bracelet and prayed for the gods to give her good luck.

Don't stop now, she said. *Get me to America. Keep this plane in the air. Don't let it fall.* She leaned against the plane's window and watched the low buildings surrounded by palm trees stretch out beneath her; next, the mountains; and then the plane ascended up through the clouds until the whole earth disappeared beneath the cloud layer.

At home, Mai had stretched out on her back on the rice paddy dyke and studied the clouds as they sailed by, so far away, so high, unreachable. And now, to look down upon them. Her head swirled.

Just then, the face with those round blue eyes poked in front of her, asking a question she didn't understand. Mai shrank back into the corner of her seat and shook her head. Whatever it was, no. *No. No. Just go away and leave me be.* The hand held a tray in front of her with a small box, filled with a piece of chicken, rice, and something green. *No.* She shook her head again, *no*. Even though she had not eaten for hours, she wasn't hungry. The pale white face with the blue eyes would not go away.

Then the mouth moved again, more strange-sounding words coming through those bright red lips. This time they were directed at the businessman next to her. He turned to Mai, smiled, and asked her in Mandarin if she would like something to drink or eat.

Surprised, she nodded. "Just water, please."

Not satisfied, he spoke to her again. "Would you like a Coke?"

A Coke. How long had it been since she'd had a Coke? She remembered the sweet syrupy taste, the dark cola color. Father had bought her one when they were in Can Tho.

"Oh, yes, yes. Thank you," she said as the man repeated her reply to the flight attendant in English. The blue eyes flashed, the red lips parted in a smile, and the woman returned with a cup of ice and a bottle of Coke. She poured it into the cup and handed it to the businessman, who passed it to Mai.

She held the cup in her hands, feeling the cold, staring at the bubbles on the surface of the dark liquid. She sipped the Coke slowly, savoring the feel of the liquid sliding down her throat. The plane leveled off. Mai finished her drink and struggled to keep her eyes open, but the effort was too much. Her shoulders sagged, her head listed to one side. A deep weariness overcame her, turning her arms and legs to limp noodles, and she was aware of nothing until the stewardess nudged her to put her seat back up. She heard a grinding sound, and felt the plane dropping from the sky.

Twenty

Did Mai's parents know she was alive? Would she ever see Kien again? What would life with Third Uncle be like? If only she knew the answers to these questions, but she didn't. And so the young girl in the red blouse with the lucky gold bracelet hidden in her pocket pressed her nose to the plane's window, her eyes searching the dark landscape for her new life. The Chinese businessman stood up, folded his newspaper on the seat, and pulled a pack of cigarettes from his shirt pocket.

"Are we there?" Mai asked him, leaning on the armrest.

"No," he replied, tapping a cigarette on the pack. "Japan. This is Tokyo, the capital. Just refueling. You can get off if you want to. I'm going to go have a smoke," he added before he turned to go.

Mai cowered in her seat. *No. No getting off. Too scary.* She'd stay in the safety of her seat, listening to the murmurs behind her, the wail of a tired child, the shuffling of feet going past her. She pressed her nose to the window again. *Hard glass. Everything blurry. Night.* A sea of city lights sequined the darkness. Her first glimpse of a big city. What was its name? Oh yes, Tokyo. She saw dark silhouettes of buildings, taller than she had ever seen before. This airport was so vast. Shadows of uniformed men moved on the tarmac.

What was Kien doing now? Was it night on the island? Was he thinking of her? Was he missing her? The love song he had strummed on the beach that moonlit night, when the stars danced and the sand sparkled, played in her head. *"You asked me how much I love you, the brightness of the moon is a symbol of my love for you."* She hummed the melody low, under her breath, burying her face in the small blue airplane pillow until the tune turned into a wail, swallowed up by the softness of the pillow.

A tap on the shoulder. Fasten your seat belt.

The businessman turned to her. "Next stop San Francisco, the United States," he said, his breath stinking of smoke. Mai shrank back from him and nodded. Father smelled like that. She buried her face in the pillow and felt the plane ascend once again. America. So far. And so big. Such strange sounding names. When would she get there? Would Third Uncle and Auntie be waiting for her? Would she recognize them? She tried to picture their faces, but all she could see was Kien, immobile on the pier, his eyes filled with sadness, his hands digging deep into the pockets of his faded blue shorts.

She dozed and dreamed that she was on the fishing trawler again, knees frozen to her chest, the stench of urine and vomit filling the hold while sea water sloshed around her, her stomach a hollow pit of hunger, the cries of frightened refugees calling out for mercy as the groaning ship rose and fell, beating its way through the white-capped waves, tossed like a child's top across the storm-filled sea, tumbling bodies, hands reaching into black nothingness for something to hold on to. A baby girl rolled from her mother's lap and fell onto her legs. She tried to save her from the water, but every time she stretched out her arms, the baby disappeared.

A cart rattled next to her. A hand touched her shoulder. The boat turned into an airplane and the tangled throng of refugees into rows of well-dressed people belted in cushioned seats. Mai rubbed her eyes and pointed to the can of Coke on the cart. The stewardess smiled, reached over and put her tray table down, and set a cup of ice and the Coke can on it. Oh, the pleasure of having a cold drink. The coolness slid down her parched desert throat, and she rolled an ice cube around on her tongue. Would the dryness in her throat every go away?

Oh no. After several sips, Mai felt pressure on her bladder, too strong to ignore. Embarrassed, she turned to the businessman next to her and asked him if the plane had a toilet. He nodded yes, pushed the small button on his arm rest, and a stewardess bustled down the aisle toward them. She smiled at Mai and motioned to her to step into the aisle. Unbuckling her seat belt, Mai brushed past the businessman, stretched out her arms to hold onto the seats, and followed the stewardess toward the back of the plane. Relief! There was no one in line. The folding door was open, and she peered in at the silver bowl. A toilet like Grandfather had installed at their house. Before that, there'd been a hole in the ground.

A piece of glass covered the wall above the sink. Back in the Malaysian airport, Mai had caught a brief glimpse of a girl in the glass, a girl who might be her, but she had turned away. Now, in the close confines of the airplane toilet, she could no longer avoid this girl, the thin, tanned, straggly-haired girl staring back at her. Moving closer, she examined her eyes. Coal black, bright. Eyes that had seen so much. She moved, and the girl in the glass moved. Mai put her hand to her chin. The girl in the glass put her hand to her chin. She stuck out her tongue at the girl in the glass. The girl in the glass stuck her tongue out at Mai. Mai put her hand on the glass and tried to touch the girl. She couldn't. She and the girl in the glass, the same.

She touched her face. So dark. Light yellow skin turned to a dark golden tan beneath the searing island sun. She'd never been allowed out in the sun without being covered; dark skin was the sign of a peasant. She tried to rub the darkness out of her skin, but it was no use. How upset Mother would be. Raising her blouse, Mai examined the light skin beneath it, the growing bumps of breasts. Could the rest of her ever be light again? She took one last look in the glass. Even her lips were brown. A sigh. She pulled her shirt down and stepped out of the tiny cubicle.

The businessman had fallen asleep, a slight snore whistling through his nostrils. Oh no. How would she get into her seat? Mai stood in the aisle and chewed on her lip. The floor of the plane started to jiggle. The stewardess came bouncing down the aisle as English words came over the loudspeaker. She motioned Mai to her seat. The businessman, awakened by the announcement, unbuckled his seat belt and stood to let Mai by.

Anxiety began to creep into her mind. Voices started to

speak to her. Ghost voices. *Do you know how high you are in the air? If this plane crashes, everyone will die. You'll never see your uncle.* What, Mai wondered, was the matter with the other passengers? Why weren't they afraid? Her stomach started to seesaw. The gold bracelet. She still had it. She reached in her pocket. Her good luck charm. She clutched it and braced herself. Just then the plane leveled off, an announcement came over the speaker system, and the seat belt sign went off

Mai closed her eyes and pretended to sleep. She couldn't wait to get to Chicago. All of her troubles would be over then. Third Uncle was her smartest uncle, and the nicest. Mai's father had given up his own opportunity for college to run the rice mills so that Third Uncle could go to college in America.

If you were rich, you went to the United States or France to college. It was hard to believe they had been rich. Third Uncle had returned after college and flown a helicopter in the South Vietnamese Army, escaping on the last one out from the roof of the American Embassy when Saigon fell to the Communists. Father, in order to protect his family, had burned Third Uncle's picture and disowned him. After he had handed him a bag of diamonds to smuggle out.

"Don't worry, Mai," Father had said. "Third Uncle will treat you like his own child. You will be walking on streets of gold."

Starved for a sense of belonging, Mai envisioned life as it had been before the war and dreamed that it would be that way again, with the whole family reunited, like the pieces of a broken rice bowl glued back together again. She pushed that letter from Third Uncle into the back of her mind, not willing to believe the hardships he'd described.

Fishing, catching cicadas and butterflies...how happy she had been at home. And would be again. But she felt tired of it all. Tired. So tired. Her limbs went limp and the plane disappeared into the darkness of sleep.

She felt an arm brush across her as morning light streamed in the plane's window.

"Look. The Golden Gate Bridge."

Raising the window shade, the businessman pointed to the longest bridge Mai had ever seen. Two bright orange, ladderlike towers reached to the blue sky, narrow strands stretching from them to the suspended roadway beneath, where lines of cars and trucks streamed in both directions, the sea swirling far beneath them. A boat, its white sails billowing in the wind, slipped beneath the bridge. Trees and mountains were one way. In the distance were tall buildings, the tallest she'd ever seen. Was everything giant-size in America?

"Skyscrapers," the businessman said. "I don't know why they build them here. Lots of earthquakes."

"Earthquakes?" said Mai, turning to him. "What are those?"

"Sometimes the ground shakes, and then the buildings fall down. Don't worry. No earthquakes now."

Why hadn't someone warned her? She'd never go up in one of those buildings. Third Uncle hadn't told her about skyscrapers. What a strange name. Did they really touch the sky? The buildings below were smaller now, more like home with their red-tiled roofs, *but look at all the cars*, she thought. Where were the motorcycles? Only the rich had cars in Vietnam.

The fog-covered San Francisco Airport unveiled itself as

Mai's plane taxied down the runway. When it had rolled to a stop, she exited the cabin, holding her breath, her shaking hands wrapped around her two bags, drops of perspiration trickling down her cheeks. Now she was breathing the air deeply, wanting to take it all in at once. The stewardess's words echoed something about TWA, and passengers brushed by her in a hurry to somewhere. Mai's eyes darted around the airport. She was dazzled by the large signs, and the shops filled with toys, books, clothing—anything you wanted was on display.

So many round white faces, blue eyes, blond hair. Black faces, dark eyes with curly hair. A stewardess hurried by, her high heels clicking against the walkway. How could she walk in those? Mai stared down at her dép. *Please don't make me wear shoes like that.*

"Miss Nguyen. Are you Miss Nguyen?" a white-skinned lady asked.

Yes, she was saying her name. Mai nodded. A voice booming over a loudspeaker echoed through the building and a buzz of voices accompanied it. Mai cringed and covered her ears.

Brown metal folding chairs, their battered seats staring at the low ceiling as if they'd been waiting forever, slouched in crooked rows in the airport room where Mai was led by the smiling, blue-uniformed woman with the blond frizzled hair. The woman reminded her of Cindy, the American English teacher. Mai tried her few words of English.

"Hello, how are you?" she said, emphasizing each syllable and doing her best to paste a wide smile across her face.

The woman, ignoring her efforts, pointed to a chair and motioned for her to sit. The metal legs creaked as Mai lowered herself onto its narrow seat while peering out of the corner of her eyes at the scene around her, listening to the scuffle of feet and the soft whispers of excitement floating like little islands. Folding her hands in her lap, her fingers tight around her bag of precious papers and the bag containing her few possessions, she glanced at her dirty toenails and her worn dép. If she curled her feet under the chair, maybe no one would notice them.

A tired Vietnamese mother, accompanied by three boys and a man Mai assumed to be her husband, sat in the chairs in front of her. The youngest child slept, his head cradled in the lap of his older brother, who did not stir. The oldest brother, who was probably about Minh's age, turned to gawk at her. When he realized she was aware of him, his head swiveled around and all Mai could see was the dark shaggy hairline on the back of his skinny neck. She lowered her eyes, trying not to stare at the family scene, the parents' heads whispering together, the boys huddled near them. How she envied them.

More refugees crept into the room until almost every chair was occupied. Several men, their eyes darting around the room, perched along the back wall. Everyone waiting for his name to be called.

A small wooden desk claimed the front center of the scene, two folding chairs on either side. Behind the desk sat a balding man with black-framed eyeglasses. Surveying the rows, he picked up a piece of paper and called out a name. Next to him, Mai could see an unsmiling Vietnamese woman, her eyebrows like upside-down Vs, her forehead filled with long striped lines. What if Mai couldn't answer their questions?

Relieved her name hadn't been called, she watched as one of the men from the back wall jumped forward and hurried to sit in the chair in front of the desk. The balding man spoke to the Vietnamese woman, the woman spoke to the refugee man, the refugee man spoke back to her, and she translated to the bald white man.

Straining to hear what they were saying, Mai's hands trembled. This was going to take forever. Who were these people? Did they have the power to decide if she could live in America?

Her teeth tore at the hangnail on her right thumb. The skin parted and a tiny pool of blood oozed to the surface. A bad habit, but one she hadn't tried to break. She hesitated and then put her lips to her thumb to clean the wound.

The refugee man rose from his seat and, clutching a fistful of papers, departed through the back doorway. The metal edges of the skinny chair cut into Mai's thighs as she watched a trail of refugees called to the small wooden desk. Finally, it was her turn. She floated to the front of the room as if in a dream, touching her gold bracelet.

My moment.

Remember it always.

Beginning. Again.

She stood frozen before the desk, eyes cast down, afraid to look up. The man grunted something to the woman, who instructed her in Vietnamese to sit. Mai reached behind her and felt for the edge of the chair as she sat, her eyes still cast down.

"Papers!" the woman said.

Pulling her papers from the plastic bag, she presented them in a disheveled stack to the balding man. He perused them, looked up, and spoke to the woman.

"One more, we need one more," she said to Mai, her eyes rock-hard behind her short eyelashes.

Please don't let me vomit. Mai's stomach rolled as she desperately groped in her bag for the missing paper. Nothing. The image of stepping back onto Pulau Tengah to spend the rest of her life there bolted through her mind. *Where is it?* As she squirmed in the chair, clawing through the bag, her toe touched something. She leaned over and grabbed the missing paper from underneath the table—she had dropped it. She presented it to the woman with both hands, as if she had discovered a bag of gold.

The woman took it without comment and handed it to the man, who pushed his glasses up his nose with his index finger and brought the paper close to his face. More questions through the interpreter; Mai held her breath after each one, choosing her words carefully, afraid to make a mistake. Then they gave her an important-looking document. It had *I-94* on it. A permanent resident alien. Nguyen Mai. No more a refugee.

"You can become a citizen in five years," the Vietnamese woman said. Finally, they gave her a plane ticket. To Chicago, the end of the journey.

The interpreter's forehead smoothed into a smile. "Chicago. That's where the world's tallest building is, the Sears Tower," she said.

Mai bowed. *I don't know what she's talking about,* she thought. *I just want to get out of here now that I've got my papers, before they change their minds and ask for something else.*

Turning to walk out the door, she heard someone call her name. "Mai?"

It was soft at first as if the speaker wasn't sure. Then it came again.

No one knew Mai here. Why was someone speaking to her? Mai looked up and locked eyes with those of a young Vietnamese woman, a startled expression on her face.

"Mai, I'm so happy to see you." The young woman moved closer and bowed, the palms of her hands pressed together.

It was Lan. What was she doing here? She was supposed to be back in Malaysia in the hospital. Mai rubbed her tired eyes to make certain they weren't deceiving her.

"Mai." Another voice. Ngoc stepped out from behind Lan and reached for Mai.

Mai was numb, happy, surprised, bewildered. Then her tears broke loose, one at a time, and there was a torrent on all three faces. Ngoc pulled Lan and Mai out the doorway into the corridor where a stream of passengers flowed by—tan young women with sun-streaked hair in tight jeans and sweaters, faces bare of makeup; businessmen in dark suits and ties clutching small leather bags; tired-looking women pushing crying babies in little carts with wheels.

Mai pulled away and stared at the other two girls. "How did you get here? I left you in Malaysia."

"The doctor. He decided it was safe for Lan to travel and made arrangements for us to leave," Ngoc said, clutching her sister's hand.

"We've just landed," Lan added, casting her eyes down. "I'm sorry I ran away without telling you goodbye." She placed her hands on her abdomen. Mai noticed two soldiers in dark blue uniforms with tiny golden wings on their jackets eyeing them.

"We were so worried about you. We thought you'd drowned. We looked all over, and then I saw you on the boat." Mai's accusing voice trailed off.

"And I saw you and waved." Lan's voice cracked. "I didn't know what to do with Hiep gone."

Mai's head dropped and her shoulders slumped as she ran her finger along the edge of her plane ticket. Looking up at the girls, she said, "I have to get on the plane for Chicago. Do you know where you're going?"

"We're going to Boston," answered Ngoc. "Our mother's sister lives there. Is Boston far from Chicago?"

"I don't know," answered Mai.

What was going to happen to Lan and the baby? How would they manage without Hiep? What would their auntie do? Mai knew that Vietnamese girls did not have babies if they weren't married. The shame. It wasn't allowed. They did something to you so that the baby died. Mai had heard the girls whispering about it in the camp and knew that Lan would need a lot of good luck to keep that baby. And a lot of money.

"Come in here with me," she said, pointing to the door with a figure of a woman on it. Lan and Ngoc followed her into a restroom with the rows of gleaming stalls.

"Wait," Mai whispered, ducking into a stall and sliding the latch on the door. Her fingers fumbled in her pocket, and she pulled out the gold bracelet. Beautiful and glistening. She didn't need it anymore. She had her plane ticket and entrance papers, but Lan and the baby, they needed it now. She would create her own luck. Would Mother and Father approve?

For the first time, Mai realized her parents' approval didn't matter. She knew what she was doing was right. Lan would need money, to live and to keep Hiep's baby. She opened the door and pulled Lan into the stall, took her friend's hand, and deposited the bracelet in her palm.

"Shh. Hide it. It's good luck, for you and the baby."

Lan's eyes grew soft. Her lip trembled as she tried to say something, but Mai shook her head.

"Please," she pleaded. "It has much good luck."

Lan slid the bracelet into her pocket and hugged Mai. Mai pushed the door open and they stepped back into the room where Ngoc, her back to them, was washing her hands in one of the silver bowls that lined the wall. She dried her hands on the brown paper towel and turned to them with a question in her eyes.

Mai exited the washroom. Someone was walking toward her, calling her name. Mai recognized the lady who had escorted her from the airplane to the refugee processing center. She was speaking rapidly in English and motioning for Mai to follow.

Turning to Lan and Ngoc, Mai cried, "How will I find you again?"

Lan scrawled a name and address on a scrap of paper

and placed it in Mai's hand. "This is my auntie's name and address. Write me when you get to your uncle's."

Mai folded the paper and tucked it in the palm of her hand. "Don't forget me, Lan. Please don't forget me. I want to see Uncle Hiep's baby."

Tears sparkling like tiny diamonds on her lashes, Lan whispered, "Don't worry, Mai. I won't forget you. We are sisters now. Nothing will change that. Goodbye."

Ngoc echoed her goodbye. No touching, no hugs, no bows.

Mai turned and followed the airline lady down a long hallway to an area where a slight young man with a snake tattoo on his bare arm was standing in line behind a short overweight woman with too-tight jeans. The airline lady motioned to Mai to join the line. The sign on the wall had a long word on it.

"What does it say?" she asked the lady.

"Chicago," she replied.

The last part of the journey. How many months had it taken to come to this place?

Mai remembered the beginning, when Hiep's hands helped her clamber onto the ship that carried them across the South China Sea. She remembered his hands pulling her out of the waves and onto the beach when they'd arrived at Pulau Tengah. And now the airline lady's hands steered her onto the plane and left her with the stewardess, who guided her to her seat.

If she closed her eyes very tightly, she could imagine herself back on the island, curled up in her hammock, the tarp above her, Hiep sleeping below her, the waves crashing, the wind blowing, the smell of the sea and the smoke from the cooking fires.

Reaching into her pocket, she closed her fingers around the space where her gold bracelet had been. She prayed for Kien, and for Lan's unborn baby. Would they all be together someday?

Outside, the sun scattered its beams through the airplane window, and the blue sky beckoned as her plane roared down the runway. Mai's fingers slipped from her pocket and she smiled. She was safe from Sang's ghost, and an orphan no more.

Author's Note

April 30, 2015, is the fortieth anniversary of the fall of Saigon. On that day in 1975, North Vietnamese troops captured the South Vietnamese capital and ended a twenty-year war between South Vietnam, supported by the U.S. and its allies, and North Vietnam, allied with Russia and China. The North Vietnamese renamed Saigon "Ho Chi Minh City," and the country of Vietnam still celebrates April 30 as Reunification Day. For the thousands of South Vietnamese who fled, and for their descendants, it was the day they lost their country and will forever be mourned as "Black April."

After the war, the new Vietnamese government enacted harsh policies, sending one to two million people to re-education camps, where over 165,000 died; 50,000 to 100,000 people were executed. Farmlands were seized and redistributed. Families were forced to leave the cities and farm in the "New Economic Zones," and the ethnic Chinese (or "Hoa") saw their businesses confiscated. Over two million South Vietnamese, who came to be known as the "boat people," fled Vietnam in overcrowded boats, their destinations Malaysia, Indonesia, Thailand, the Philippines, Singapore, and Hong Kong. According to the United Nations High Commission for Refugees, 200,000 to 400,000 died at sea.

It is estimated that of the 800,000 boat people who survived, more than half were resettled in the United States; the rest found refuge in France, Canada, Australia, Germany, and the United Kingdom. Many were tragically repatriated to Vietnam.

Acknowledgments

My friend, Huong Banh, is a Vietnamese boat person. Without her, I could not have written this book. She shared her experiences with me, read the manuscript, and offered suggestions. Though the characters in this book are fictional, the historical background and circumstances are real.

I would also like to thank Fred Shafer, who believed I could write this novel and edited and shepherded me through the process. The input of the writers in his Sunday night novel group was invaluable. To the Off Campus Writers Workshop and the members and speakers who encourage and inspire me every week, I thank you. To my incredible agent, Tina P. Schwarz, who brought my manuscript out of the drawer and into the world, and to my editors at Flux, Brian Farrey-Latz and Sandy Sullivan, along with everyone at Flux who shaped it for publication, thank you. Grateful appreciation to my friend, Todd Musburger, for his legal expertise, and to my family: Mark who helped with computer problems, Beth who read early chapters, and Mike who critiqued the entire manuscript several times and offered valuable advice. Also to Dinah and Suzanna for their encouragement, and to my parents for instilling in me the love of literature. And most of all, to my ever-patient husband, Ray, who has helped me every step of the way.

About the Author

Joyce Burns Zeiss has always wanted to be a writer. After retiring from teaching junior high school, she became a member of the Off Campus Writers Workshop in Winnetka, Illinois. Her experiences resettling a Chinese Cambodian refugee family in 1979 and her subsequent trips to work in refugee camps in Africa fueled her interest in the plight of the refugee. Her first novel, *Out of the Dragon's Mouth*, is based on the true-life experiences of a fellow teacher who fled Vietnam as an adolescent to cross the South China Sea in the hold of a fishing boat. To learn more, visit her website at www.joyceburnszeiss.com.